AF347044

Friends with Summer

JYOTI SINGH

LITERATURESLIGHT PUBLISHING

Near collectorate, Pathak Colony,
Jashpur Nagar, Chhattisgarh 496331
www.literatureslight.com

Copyright ©, 2021, Jyoti Singh

All Rights Reserved

ISBN: 978-81-950945-7-8

This book has been published with all reasonable efforts taken to make the material error-free after the consent of the author. No part of this book may be reproduced, transmitted, or stored in a retrieval system, in any form or by any means, electronic, mechanical, magnetic, optical, manual, photocopying, or otherwise, without permission in writing from the author.

The opinions/ contents expressed in this book are solely of the author and do not represent the opinions/ standings/ thoughts of Literatureslight.

Acknowledgements

Behind every success, big or small, there is a lot of effort made by many unsung heroes who recognize, help and motivate a person to become who they are. I am tremendously lucky to have had such people backing me and I would love to express my gratitude to them.

I have to thank my parents who provided me with the best of everything that they had and even more.

Thank you Papa for believing that I could do something. You inspired me to write. You don't know that you did. You're missed.

Thank you Mummy for letting me be myself and for showing me how to power through any situation. You taught me to hold my head high.

Thank you brother for being the light of my life.

I'm deeply grateful for all my Gurus— Thank you to Mr. D.V. Singh Sir, a living legend whose teachings were vital in helping me to understand and become any good at English. I still have a long road to go, I know.

Thank you Monika Saxena Mam, Nelofer Mam, Kadambari Mam and Toshi Mam for being the absolute queens that you are. You always motivated me and made me see the good about myself that even I wasn't aware of.

Amrish Chaturvedi Sir, thank you for being kind and for making Mechanical Engineering easier for me to deal with during my toughest time.

Thank you Pradeep Gupta Sir for believing in me. You told me, in front of a whole audience that I was going to do great. It was such a blessing.

There was one more teacher, an absolute angel she was to me. Unfortunately, I don't remember her name because I was a really small kid back then. I used to suck at writing, so much so that I hated to even hold a pencil properly. She taught me how to write properly. She was the one who made me believe that discipline and perfection could be achieved with love. She stood up to my bullies. Thank you Mam, I don't remember your name but I remember you.

This acknowledgement is incomplete without thanking my friends who have seen me through my lowest and never stopped supporting me. Thank you Ayushi, Namrta, Krati, Kusum, Kasim, Prateek and someone else whose name I can't use for privacy reasons. You guys are awesome.

A big thank you to Literature's Light for helping and guiding me patiently through the tedious process of publishing my dream project.

Lastly and most importantly, thank you God.

Dedication

This book is dedicated to you, my reader and God who has been helping me all my life in his own ways. I truly wish from my heart that you thoroughly enjoy reading it as much as I enjoyed the process of visualising (the cover and the storyline), contemplating, writing and revising it. It's been an honour.

This book proved to be a personal milestone for me. It transformed me in ways that nothing ever could. I guess that's what happens when you choose to follow your true heart's desire, your passion and that is one of the bravest things one could do.

I say so because your heart might ask you to go against the grain. It might ask you to challenge every notion that you have ever had of yourself and the society. It might ask you to be a completely different person than who you have been all your life.

And if you still choose to follow it, it will take you home to your truest self that's forever free.

Keep doing what you believe in and life will unfold like a brand new discovery, every single day. That's the magic of following your heart.

Be happy, be kind, love yourself and enjoy!

This is a work of fiction. Names, characters, businesses, places, events, locales, and incidents are products of the author's imagination. Any resemblance to actual persons, living or dead, or actual events is purely coincidental.

Some parts of the book might not be suitable for children and teenagers. Parental guidance is advised.

Table of Contents

I dare you to believe in yourself.

Chapter 1

ROUTINE

*O*h damn... It's morning...

Oh! It's morning!!

I'm going to have a great day...

Yes, Ray! We're going to have a great day today.

She woke up from the bed unwillingly, turned the light on and looked at herself in the mirror.

A diamond shaped face, a wheatish complexion which was glowing after the sleep, defining eyebrows with a pair of jet black eyes matching her medium length black hair and a new pimple that she ignored and gave the mirror a big smile. A smile that was admired by many, she was told so.

Ray entered the bathroom lousily and tried to keep her head upright. Smiling again forcibly, she lifted the toothbrush. She decided that she was going to bathe today. Although she knew that it should be done everyday, she thought it was okay to skip a day in between.

Ray got dressed up hastily, in whatever clothes that she could first lay her hands on and took a quick look in the mirror but she was not satisfied. Her hair was still undone but again, she forced a smile on her face and left for work.

It was actually a fifteen minute drive from her room but obviously, it had to be extended by another ten courtesy of traffic jam. Her stomach was growling because she didn't have any breakfast.

Great! No breakfast today again. Now I'll just have to have something from the cafeteria.

"Whyyy?!" she cried. Ray looked out of the window of her car to catch the reflection of a guy in his rear-view mirror. He was in the driver's seat of a car ahead of hers. His dark hair was in striking contrast with the skin and his facial features were *just fine,* Ray decided. Then, she noticed his car which was a humble micro.

Oh... such a cutie, can make any car look better!

she thought.

"Oh well." Ray pulled her attention back into her hatchback and accelerated the car ahead as the signal turned green.

She noticed from the corner of her eye that the guy was now noticing her. Ray smiled to herself victoriously and then immediately, calmed herself down.

It was not unusual for her to get looks like that but she always got too excited about little things. And now, she was smiling all the way to her office. It had made her day.

"It's not that hard. See?" she said to herself.

I just have to smile more and I'll be fine.

Have to?

No. I smile more... naturally.

That's more like it.

And she felt a shiver go down her body. Ray used to catch feels quite easily but she was careful enough to not let it show. Not everyone will understand and they might think that she is moody. That was the reason why she preferred to spend time by herself. It was the only time when she could be in her feelings; unjudged and unseen.

There was one more person who she felt unjudged by but she had pushed him somewhere in the closet of her mind and as Ray remembered that, his face came to her and she felt relaxed.

She parked the car and stepped out to take a look at the cars in the parking lot. Found her second hand hatchback to be averagely fitting amongst the SUVs, Crossovers and Sedans.

Oh well, at least I have a four-wheeler.

And her mind started playing the images of not just all of her friends but everyone she knew. One by one, she satisfied herself with the thought that most of them did not own a car. Ray felt a little delighted and more vexed due to the fact that her friends were not so rich. But she also knew that they cared for her and will be there whenever she needed them.

So, Ray smiled to herself when no one was looking. She looked at herself in the glass door and opened it, giving a smile to a stranger coming through and punched herself in.

Chapter 2

HI BOSS!

Ray was three minutes early today. Went in to catch eyes with Mohit.

Mohit was just a colleague as per her own thinking but she knew he had slightly different feelings for her. He was a stout guy with wavy hair. His nose was a little bigger than usual but his face was even bigger. His eyes, small and brown, protected by glasses.

On her first day in the company, D-Ginnie, he was assigned as her mentor and she was seated next to him incase she needed any help.

"Here," Mohit had said. She moved her head away from the computer screen, looked at the coffee she was being offered and accepted it with a smile— "Thanks!" and returned back to her work immediately. Mohit took good care that she never got too serious and kept cracking jokes every now and then.

"Don't worry, your mother-in-law isn't waiting at home for you to do the dishes."

Ray made a face of half-disgust.

"Oh come on, why do you take so much pressure? Chill..."

Ray could not suppress her smile anymore. Mohit's jokes were nowhere near funny to her but the fact that he cared and that he was so confident and almost smug about delivering them shitty jokes, made her laugh. And that's why she spent her breaks with him. Because yes, he made her laugh. It was an easy friendship.

Like every other day, she sat on her usual chair and turned her computer on and from the edge of her desktop, she saw a silhouette coming towards the door. She instantly straightened her legs and back and continued typing. It was the director, Miss Viyona who had walked in and instantly, the whole energy of the room changed.

Viyona was a charming lady in her late thirties. Her eyes were piercing through her round glasses, catching every detail of the room while she gave smiles to anyone she met eyes with.

Viyona was five-eight with a defined and sculpted figure which was even more highlighted by her suit. Perhaps she intended it that way. She wore her highlited hair in a high ponytail and the guys were grateful for her visits in the office apparently. She might as well be a model and the girls looked up to her. For she was quite accomplished for her age.

No doubt, she was charming but there was something that she used to hide behind her squinted eyes, Ray always felt that. Viyona's eyes met Ray's and she smiled back instantly.

Too eager,

she chided herself and released an audible sigh which she hoped, nobody had heard.

Viyona went into her cabin but she was going to return for a group talk later on. Everyone knew that.

***

"Hello my knights and dames! Hope you all are well today," Viyona addressed the seventy-seven people in the room.

"Yes mam!" said Daisy too early, a newbie at D-Ginnie, who was only a month old in the company. She held her tongue between her teeth regrettingly.

"That's the spirit Daisy, but you can call me Viyona. Simple. Okay?" she said, again smiling with too squinted eyes that beamed through her glasses. Daisy smiled back too eagerly, shrugging her shoulders.

"Well, as you guys know that it's been a phenomenal month for our company and that is all because of our heroes and that's you guys so, give yourselves a huge, huge round of applause."

Everyone clapped with her.

Ray was smiling and clapping while contemplating what she was going to say next.

"... And the best part is that we've exceeded our target by four folds! Isn't that freakishly awesome guys?"

"WOO! YES!" someone shouted from the back and everyone started hooting.

"And." Viyona commanded silence and continued, "And as a result, guys here's the big news, D-Ginnie is the biggest digital marketing company in the country! Yes, guys, we are the biggest in our country!" she exclaimed, her hands in the air.

A roar busted out of the crowd and the whole energy of the room went from anticipatory to euphoric within a moment.

"And that's the reason why we've decided to organize a big party on Friday night!" she announced.

"But before that, it is only befitting that we show some love and support for the people who have worked exceptionally hard to make our dream more than achievable. So today, I'll be more than happy to announce their names," she said cheerfully.

"So that's it, some of us are going to get their raises today," said Mohit.

"Oh come on, that's a far-fetched statement. You know that's not going to happen. I've been waiting for mine for six years now," said Santosh Saab.

Santosh Saab was a smiley person in his late fifties. He was the most adequately dressed too, in his neatly buttoned safari suit and shiny shoes. A little belly bump could be seen. His hair was still very much black and full, always oiled and he had this habit of scratching his nose every now and then.

Viyona continued, "I'll be calling out some names and after that, the called out employees may move straight to the HR manager's cabin. And the names are... Santosh Saab!"

Santosh Saab instantly twitched his nose and rushed to get a picture with Viyona, his eyes gleaming.

"Congratulations, Santosh Saab. As we all know he's the most dedicated and experienced employee in our company, so give a huge round of applause to Santosh Saab!"

She did not shake hands with Santosh Saab but gave him a tight, side hug. Santosh Saab eloped into the HR manager's cabin.

"That wasn't very obvious," said Mohit sarcastically.

"Don't act like you didn't know," Ray teased him.

"You're going to be the next, miss."

"Yeah sure..." she said, tossing out the compliment.

One by one, names were announced and the whole consortium was coming to an end.

"So guys, before we wrap up, I'd finally like to highlight some other names too who have done excellent work. So here are our stars... Rayveena, Shubh, Mohit and Lily," She took the names in one breath.

"Thank you Viyona!" said Shubh, Mohit and Lily together.

"It's all because of your guidance and leadership," said Ray with her hands clasped together to her chest.

"Yes, that's right," the other three nodded.

Viyona gave them a thumbs up.

Chapter 3

FAMILY

"Hi mom," Ray said cheerfully as the line connected. "Hello..? Are you there?" Silence on the other side continues for a moment.

"Ya hello, I was just picking up laundry, there are so many clothes."

"Oh okay," replied a meek voice.

A deathly silence continued.

Why does she always do this? Can't she just talk to me normally?

She released an audible sigh and continued, "So... hum... what did you have for dinner today?" while tapping her fingers on the bed.

"O nothing else that same usual beans. Your father and I thought that we should finish the leftovers. What did you have?"

"Nothing else, I had the same." And silence. "What is dad doing?" she forced out.

"He's watching news."

"Well, I only called to tell you something." Ray felt her cheeks go red.

"Oh God! Are you trying to make the whole world deaf? Turn the volume down a little bit," Mom rebuked dad. "Yes? You were saying something?"

"Nothing."

"Oh come on tell me, I was just—"

"I know, I heard you."

"Then tell me."

"Um, well today our director informed us that our company has become the best in the country."

"That's good news! So are they giving you a raise now?"

Ray felt her heart sink. "Um... no, they're giving raises to the more experienced ones."

"I see."

"But the director mentioned my name today, for my performance."

"Of course she would, you always work so hard for no reason."

"For no reason?"

"Yes, why do you bother so much? We have everything here for you."

"Mom, you don't understand."

"Arrey?! For how long will you do that fruitless job? Come back home and we'll get you married to a nice guy who'll take care of you. You won't have to do a thing. Your parents know what's good for you. Like our parents knew what's good for us."

"But you always say that your life is ruined because your marriage was arranged with dad," Ray said blatantly.

"So you're never going to listen to us? Fine, do as you please."

"Why do you always get so hyper? There's a time for everything."

"So just tell me when is your time to get married?"

"I don't know," said Ray, irritated.

"That's great! For how long will I keep listening to the world. What should I tell them when they ask me when my daughter is getting married?"

"It's none of their business and besides that I'm only twenty mom!" She almost shouted.

"Do you know how old I was when I got married?"

"Mom, I'm not going to repeat your mistakes." She let out a defeated sigh. "Mom, I really should sleep. I'm really tired. I'm hanging up."

"Okay."

Ray held her head in her hands and curled up her toes unconsciously. She felt her breath getting faster. A pain pulsating in the arms. She reached for herself and held her own tightly.

No, I'm happy, I'm healthy, I'm fine.

She felt a pain starting on the left side of her chest.

"I just have to breathe deeply."

Ray tried to focus on her breath but the pain continued.

I'm fine. It'll be fine. No, it can't be a heart disease. I'm too young to have one. I'm too young!

What if I have to live with it all my life?

No, even if it is, it's just a very, very small part of it.

Another stinging in chest.

Should I call someone?

No, how will I explain it to them? I just have to be patient. It'll go. I'm happy. I'm healthy. I'm vibrant. I'm helpless.

No. I'm healthy. I'm happy.

Her phone rang. It was Mohit.

No. I don't want to talk to anyone right now.

She dismissed the call.

Maybe I should take the pills.

No! It's not good for me to make a habit out of it.

Suddenly, she realized that her breath had gotten shallower.

No, I can't take it. Please God, stop it. Please.

Ray come on. Breathe. Keep breathing.

Ray stood up abruptly, went for the pill, popped it into her mouth at once and drank water out of her mug. She knew it will take a few minutes before she calms down. So she opened the cupboard and removed all the clothes in it and climbed up into it.

It was a place where strangely enough, she felt safe and okay. Ray closed the doors of the cupboard as much as she could from the inside but some light from the streetlight, had still managed to come in. She kept staring at the rays until the storm inside her subsided and she fell asleep.

Chapter 4

FLASHES AND RHYTHM

"My Lord! it's 8:50!?" Ray leapt out of the night stay of her cupboard, took a quick glance in the mirror and ran towards the bathroom.

"Wait a minute!" She halted.

"It's Friday! The party! Oh great..!" she cried.

"I have nothing to wear. But I have no time to even think!"

She hurried to find something qualified for a party from the pile on the floor but let out a sigh in defeat.

I'm going to be late anyway, so why not get dressed tastefully. But if I looked too good, everyone's going to think that I got late because I was getting ready! Ugh! Damn it!

Ray decided that she was going to wear a usual top with her best jeans that always worked and to keep her hair down.

It's better to take the metro today.

She took the latest one and immediately sat on that one empty seat that every entering girl had her eyes on. She had outraced the six of them. Feeling almost sorry for them, she looked at the clock on the platform it was showing 9:25 a.m.

Oh well!

she thought loudly.

Ray immediately pulled out her lipstick from her bag and put on a tiny amount of it. She thought of putting on some eye liner too.

Where is it? It has to be here.

She looked for the eyeliner patiently and found it.

You looked better the last time I put you on,

she said to the eyeliner telepathically and remembered that it was a party at home at which she had last put it on. Flashes of her home and family started to pour into her head, uninvited. She shook her head lightly, being aware of the crowd and tried to put on the eyeliner. But it seemed too far-fetched to even try to do that in the presence of that much of kinetic energy.

***

Ray ran towards the office entrance and saw that the decorations were being done. She punched in; fifteen minutes late, hurried in and took to her seat.

"Oh, you're here."

"Hi Mohit," she released a long sigh. "It was a close call today. I don't think Viyona is here yet?"

"No."

"Thank God."

"You didn't pick up my call last night? I thought you must have slept."

Ray read his face and remembered this tiny bit of information from the heavy night that never seemed to end. "Yeah... I'm really sorry I was pretty tired. A lot of laundry you know," she tried to lie swiftly.

"Okay... by the way, I was only asking about whether you were going to attend the party or not." A little smile appeared on his face that he tried to hide but couldn't.

"Why wouldn't I? You didn't want to?" she said with a weird face.

"Yeah… I get bored easily."

*… And **my** coming here would make it fun for him? LOL.*

"Yeah, me too," she said. It was a lie. Ray loved parties because that was when she could wear dresses and look good, the best actually, in the room. But today was different. Just like several other times in the past. She felt that sinking in the chest again. Ray put her hand on her heart for a brief moment and started typing with all the muscle she could muster up.

Hours went by and finally, it was time to punch out.

"Okay guys, this is the moment that we've all been waiting for right?" Viyona said in a high pitch which was higher than her usually high pitch. She was impeccably dressed in a black georgette ethnic gown.

"Right!" everyone replied.

"We have the one and only DJ Cat Eye with us. So let's start the music. Miss DJ, shall we?"

"Well, well, there's no time to waste and the task for today, is to party harder than you work!" said Cat Eye into her mic. "Here we go!"

And the lights went dim and the music louder.

Oh well, it's not that bad now,

Ray thought to herself loudly after examining her chest by breathing in.

A little partying hurt nobody, I'm going to enjoy with all these people,

she decided.

Ray joined the dance floor and started to feel the beat. As she was getting the hang of it, she saw Mohit, standing alone.

"Aren't you going to join us?" Ray shouted.

"Yeah, come over," said the others. Mohit smiled and sighed. He joined in, almost running and taking long strides.

"I like this song," shouted Mohit.

"Then dance like it," shouted Ray. And Mohit started making waves and twisting his elbows and wrists like the Pharaohs of the Ancient Egypt. Everyone around him started cheering for him.

Ray was laughing and dancing with her best moves. She remembered the dance competitions in her school days where she could never control herself under the hypnosis of the beat. It always got to her. Now she was here; looking at the flashes, feeling the rays on her skin. She was getting eerily seduced by the night. It didn't matter to her what had happened last night. It didn't matter…

Ray was getting drunk with the darkness, the flashes, the wind, her hair flying freely, the heat of her own body, the euphoria. She never drank but here she looked like she did. Ray was absolutely drunk in the moment and wanted to make the most of it. Suddenly, a face flashed out from her memory. A countenance so soft it stroked her soul like a baby feather; whose mere memory brought something alive in her. Just a moment ago she had everything.

She was alive. Now she realized she was not so alive after all.

Viyona, out of nowhere, joined in the fun. Pursing her lips, dipping her feet in the floor and poking fingers in the sky. Everyone in the group including Ray, cheered and started doing the same. After a while, they all joined in a circle putting arms on each others' shoulders and moved their bodies together like daises do when the wind strokes them left and right.

Ray was extra-conscious now because Viyona was right on her right. She saw that Viyona had a little bit of belly today which she had never noticed before and that without her glasses, she was actually a plain-looking woman who seemed more charming because of her playful mannerisms. The employees seemed to worship this woman who was dancing right beside her. In her own case, Ray was not a devotee but a foxy observer yet deeply respectful. She knew Viyona always had her antenna up around people. Even when she is partying. Viyona was a marketing aficionado and a connoisseur when it came to people. Naturally, Ray was intimidated.

"Why do you look so stressed? Come on Rayveena, it's a party!!" Viyona said, upon finding her lost in her head.

Ray gave a big smile and nodded.

***

Almost everyone was leaving now.

"It's really late. Do you want me to drop you off?" asked Mohit.

"O I totally forgot! I didn't drive here today." She facepalmed.

"You didn't drink today, did you?" He teased.

"As a matter of fact, I never do."

"Okay then, still I can drop you off."

"No, you don't need to bother. I'll take the metro. It's alright." She started walking.

"Oh come on, I won't kidnap you."

"Excuse me? Don't even think of that. I have a lot of people behind me. They'll know."

"Like who?"

"Won't tell you."

"Okay, okay." Mohit laughed. "Come on in now," He opened the car door for her.

***

"Thank you so much…" Ray got out and closed the door with some effort.

"Anytime." He smiled. "So, what are you doing on the weekend?"

"Um, I didn't think about it. Guess I'll go and visit my family." Ray forced out the word 'family'. Still, she hoped that she sounded reasonable and believable.

"That's great. You should." He sure was a little disappointed.

"Yeah."

"Okay then, see you."

"Sure."

Ray knew that he had noticed that she was not talking much. She could be more entertaining. But she did not want to. Not today, **not with him**. Still, she gave him a gleaming and convincing smile because she did not want to be a bitch. A smile fixes everything.

Chapter 5

IN LOVE WITH WINTER

What looks good but feels even better?

Love.

Oh! to see an eternity, in a mortal just like me.

Out of nowhere, it began to sprinkle. The sky filled with thick, inky cotton. The icy wind breezed and danced about. One moment a gust, another still, like a cat ready to pounce.

The trees clattering softly and stopping suddenly, on either side of the tread. People chatting, now packing their things to leave for the safety and warmth of their homes. Nothing could be heard but the whisper and roaring and silence of the wind.

"It's so beautiful," Ray breathed, seeping in that cold winter afternoon. Just then, a sweet little vortex swished and kissed her cheeks. She closed her eyes and offered her face to the caressing of the gentlest of water droplets.

"Winters are the death of me," she said, amused.

"Like you are," said the gentlest voice of a man she ever heard.

"Like what?" She looked at him curiously.

"Like you are the death of me," he said looking into her soul.

For a moment she said nothing, letting the words resonate till the last cell of her existence; too lost in his afterglowlike eyes.

Those big brown eyes, holding an ocean of kindness. She always tried to find something in that abyss. Perhaps the pearls in his memories, the stirrings of his mind; or perhaps the weight of existence? A face as tan as the dusk. His thin lips guarding a thousand thoughts. Rounded eyebrows perfectly claimed his eyes. Hair curly and meandering towards the edges. A countenance of a lost angel and that of a warrior at the same time.

They were standing hand in hand. Ray looking up her shoulder and he looking down his, to meet each other's eyes. She gently rubbed her nose with his once.

"Oh come on," he said.

"What?" she laughed knowing what he was thinking.

"I thought we were—"

"—going to kiss?"

He made a grumpy face.

"We're in public right now, Neil." Emphasis on his name.

"Ya ya, I know, I know. I understand." He gave her a wink and a sweet smile.

"I know you do," she said with an earnest face.

"It's going to drizzle down anytime now," she said, disheartened.

"Yeah... I know," he said looking at the sky, disheartened.

"We should leave now."

"Yeah Ray, in a moment. Here, come with me." He held her hand steadily and gently got her seated on a park chair under a royal poinciana after brushing away the fallen flowers with his hand.

He sat beside her. She put her head on his shoulder near to his heart. He held her firmly within his arms. Everyone else was gone by now.

They kept gazing at the falling flowers, at the swaying of the trees; breathing in deep, the serene cold. All of it, strangely, seemed to be in sync with the rhythm of their hearts. Like this moment was surreptitiously planned and revealed by some force, only for the two of them.

"It's not real, is it?" she breathed.

"I don't know. Maybe not."

"We're dreaming, Neil."

He held her closer.

A bloaty drop fell on the periphery of his eye and he blinked several times.

"Here it goes..." he laughed. She laughed with him, nodding. And it started to pour silently. The wind had rested by then. The fernlike leaves became their brolly. "You're so beautiful," he breathed to himself.

She lifted her head up from his shoulder, met her nose with his and said, "You make me beautiful."

Her eyes again, searching for something in his. He was looking at her breathless. His heart, dropped and lost, in her being somewhere.

"What's wrong Neil?" She looked at him concerned.

"I... I don't know."

"Tell me."

"I... can't lose you." He still looked in pain.

"You won't." She assured him with all her love, putting his face in her hands. "We are together and we'll be, okay?"

"Okay." He grabbed her head gently. She held on to his arms with all the life in her being. Nothing else existed but a music in the air. A music that only they heard in each other's presence. The music that had halted the existence of time and the world both inside and outside.

"I love you."

"I love you." And he pulled her from the grasp of the universe to himself.

She surrendered to her love for him and let... everything... go...

He touched his lips on hers and a spark went blazing through them. Their lips resting on each other for a spell that was outside the grasp of time. And again that spark rose from their beings to their snug lips bringing one, unified soul of love to life. Their lips wanted to be closer than they already were, trying to suck something that could not be defined but the soul sated only with that essence. Their bodies would arise like a phoenix and got burned to ashes again. She pulled herself from him partly. He caught his breath.

"I love you."

"I love you."

Chapter 6

BEST FRIENDS' SECRETS

"Hey it's me!" Ray beamed immediately as Sanya picked the call. Sanya was her best friend since eighth standard. She was always shorter than her back then, but now she had grown into a gorgeous curvy young woman with big black eyes, chubby face, long, straight black hair and dark skin.

"Oh my Ray… how are you? Everything good?" Sanya reflected back Ray's beam.

"I'm good, what about you? It's been a while since you called. So I thought, I should check up on you."

"I know girl. I was just going to call you. I get worked up sometimes, that's it, you know."

"How's your mother doing?"

"She's doing good. What could go wrong with her?"

"You seem upset?" Ray cleared her throat immediately.

"Do I? No girl, there's nothing like that it must be the exhaustion from studying."

"Hey, Sans, don't you lie to me. I know you've been going through a tough time after—" Ray stopped herself.

"My parents divorced." Sanya completed after her.

Ray sensed the pain in her voice even though she was masquerading it with indifference.

Sanya continued, "I mean it's nothing right? It's not like they're teenagers. They're adults and know what's best for them."

"But you're not too grown up yourself Sans, are you?"

Sanya let out a sigh. A sigh that a lost somebody lets out when he has been found. A sigh of strange relief that comes when someone sees you despite all your facades.

"I... uh... I try to be positive about it," Sanya sniffed.

"You're so strong Sans, I wish I was as strong as you are."

"Oh come on, we all know what you had to do to be where you are now."

"Yes, I had to do that but there's no denying that you're so accepting of your parents." Ray empathized with her and changed the course of the conversation immediately.

Sanya knew. She played along, "I'm not as accepting as you think of me Ray. Sometimes, I can't sleep at night without waking up from a nightmare."

"When did it happen last?"

"Just last night. I don't even want to talk about it."

"What did you see?" Ray said, ignoring her pleading.

"Well, it was er... very... not your typical ghastly, claustrophobic or moore-like nightmare."

"Go on."

"It had no dreary stuff at all."

"Mm hmm?"

"It only had my mom and dad and me."

"What happened? Oh God! These neighbors." Ray had to break the focus on Sanya to complain about the banging music. She thudded her fist on the wall a couple of times and the volume lowered conveniently.

"What happened?" Sanya had to ask.

"Oh nothing girl, did you hear the music? It was so damn loud. You know how girls are here. But don't worry, I handled it. Yeah, so tell me now."

"What?"

"About your dream, silly Sans," Ray chided her.

"Yeah... so... um... me and my dad were standing in our living room and we didn't exchange any words."

"What happened next?"

"And he was staring at something."

"What?"

"At the door, and he was frozen looking at it. Like his skin had become ice itself. His fingers were trembling."

"Oh God, why?"

"I looked at the door to find out and—"

"And?"

"Mom was there with... with a man but I didn't know him. They were standing hand in hand and about to leave."

"Oh."

"Yes. And suddenly, mom turned her face to me and gave a sly smile. Like, she had defeated me or something. And she continued to scowl."

“What? Then?”

“I couldn't take her look and woke up perspiring.”

“Oh dear Sans, it must be a fear of yours. Like, you would hate to see your mom with someone else other than your father. I know any child would. So perhaps that fear in your subconscious played out in the dream. It's nothing to worry about.”

“It wasn't just a dream Ray.”

“Oh come on. Nothing like that is going to happen,” Ray told her superficially even though she knew it could happen now that Sanya's parents were divorced.

“No, Ray. I didn't tell you this, I didn't even tell my dad about it. How could I? I couldn't muster up the balls to do it Ray. I swear.”

“Hey! Hey, hold up. Calm down, easy, take a deep breath and then tell me what happened. Promise I won't judge you.” Ray prepped herself to hear the worst.

“My mom was having an affair before the divorce.”

Ray went silent trying to figure out what to say to her but she was lost for words. She breathed heavily on the phone so that Sanya knew she was still there. “I... I don't know what to say Sans, I mean—”

“It's okay Ray. You don't have to say anything. My dad knew that man, or he thought he knew him. Him and my dad used to play tennis every weekend. I had no idea.”

“God, Sans, you don't have to tell me everything.”

“But strangely enough, he'd visit us on some weekdays too, after my dad had gone for work. I was too occupied with my studies to check up on what he was doing there. Or maybe, I didn't want to see. He was very friendly with me too so I didn't know if I should say anything to him. He'd come home and I, from inside of my room, would hear them, chatting. And then one day, I didn't hear them talking. I called for mom several times, but I heard back only that creepy and eerie silence. I went out to look for them."

"Hey, it's okay Sans, have some breath. Easy."

"Nobody was in the living room. I thought they must've gone to the backyard for whatever reasons and I departed back for my room. On my way back, I saw them in the kitchen, chatting together, too close. I was getting furious because she hasn't been answering me even when she was right here, *with him.* I stood there for a minute, hoping they'd catch me watching. But it didn't happen Ray, they never looked at me. I called her one more time. Nobody answered. They both were right there in front of me and they totally denied my voice, my anger and my existence *and my father's.*"

There was a deafening silence on the phone, like a vacuum. No sound in both their brains, no sound on their lips, no sound on the phone; no ripple in the well of emotions. For a while, there was absolutely nothing that was felt .

"I can't believe this Sans."

"I couldn't either. I couldn't tell my dad. How could I? I mean in what words could I tell him?"

"Don't blame yourself dear, it's not your fault."

"That's what I keep telling myself but if I had told him before, maybe he wouldn't be so hurt after finding it out himself."

"Either way, you couldn't have stopped them from separating, Sans."

"Yes, you're right."

"Don't put pressure on yourself, they used to fight a lot anyway so perhaps, it's better for both of them."

"You're right Ray, they're grown ups, they know what's better for **them**."

"No matter what happens, I am always there for you, always with you. We're friends right?"

"Right," Sanya said beamingly. She continued, "Did you hear from him?"

"Who?" Ray pretended to not know the answer.

"Neil."

As soon as Ray heard his name, she felt her breath go slower and his face... that angel's face, hovered in her mind's eye.

Suddenly, she collected herself and said, "No." A straightforward and heavy "No." Ray started to feel a pinch in her chest and she, wanting to escape, blurted out, "Anyway, if you have any problem or anything, you can always call me, anytime. All you need to do is to have a good nap number. Okay Sans?"

"Yes, you're right girl. We'll meet soon."

"Definitely, love you Sans."

"Love you girl, bye."

"Bye, take care."

Chapter 7

HEART'S AILMENT

Ray got up from her bed and poured herself a glass of water. She was a little hung over by the conversation.

"Sanya's going to be alright," she encouraged herself and held the glass high in her hand.

"Cheers!" She gave a toast to herself in the mirror and closed her eyes and quaffed the water dearly as if it were a glass of fine Pinot Noir.

"Now, let me take a good nap number myself," she declared to the four walls of her chamber. She leapt onto the bed again, turned on the air conditioning and drew the blanket over her body self.

"God, nooo!!" Ray facepalmed and whimpered. Sis had forgotten to turn off the lights. She leapt out from the bed with God speed, got done with the deed and was back home in no time, defying the consequences of the Theory of Special Relativity.

She smiled to herself, feeling proud. It was time to drift off to the realm of dreams. She adjusted herself into her favorite position which was lying on her back, fully covered, only her face and hands out to feel the tingles from the cold air and relaxed in her body.

Now, some uninvited thoughts had the chance to show up in her consciousness. Images from that dark night flashed back, when she had safely placed herself in her cupboard.

How silly!

This night was definitely better than that one.

I hope I don't develop a heart ailment.

No, never. I'm way too young.

And she started to attend to herself.

Then what about that pain in the chest? Should I talk to the doctor about it?

No. I'm never taking those pills of half-death ever again.

Should I tell my parents? Mom at least?

What are they going to do? Remember how they threw you out of the house because of your 'drama'?

Ray felt something dissolving in her chest and she remembered that fateful night...

"I'm done with your drama. Who doesn't have problems? That doesn't mean that you get yourself tied to the bed for eternity. Do you have any idea of how much of a headache you've become to your mother and me? Can't you just be normal?" Her father shouted at a crying Ray.

Her mother looked equally irate.

He had a face so vexed and ragged that Ray was almost hateful but frightened at the same time. Hateful, because of her own family had failed to understand her plight. Frightened, because she feared that they might get her forcefully married to a stranger before time.

Ray ran towards her room, wiping tears but they never ceased. With her eyes gone blood, she hid herself in her blanket and closed her eyes to draw away from a reality that was darker than shut eyes. She tried to comfort her trembling body.

It's going to be alright. I'm fine.

But don't they see you? You're falling and falling and they won't listen to you,

a voice in her head retaliated. It goes on…

Are these your parents? Your family?

I know, I'm alone. What else can I expect?

What's the point of living such a life.

Life? I don't even know what that is. I can't believe they're my real parents. I have nowhere to go. I wish grandma was alive. Why can't they understand? I've tried to control it but it's not always possible. But God knows that I tried. God knows.

Your parents aren't Gods Ray, don't expect them to understand this when they haven't before. Ever.

Yes, that's true.

"Your life is a joke!" the masculine authority barbed from outside of her room.

"We have done everything for you. What's one thing that you don't have? You name it and we bring it to you. All this money we spent to bring you up even when you're a girl and this is what you give back to us?" the maternal authority's voice followed.

"I can't help it!" Ray screamed her lungs out. Nobody heard her.

"We even got you that high-priced treatment from that goddamned psychiatrist, and now you don't even want to take those goddamned pills?" Ray's mother yelled so loud even the neighbours heard it.

"It's because I was not able to feel anything, my mind and my body had become numb, my hands would tremble, I couldn't walk straight, I was a walking dead body," Ray cried her lungs out. She was having a panic attack.

"I say, you get out of the house! Who are you? What have you done for anyone? And you talk back like this? I see only one solution, you are getting married as soon as possible. There's no use for you here. We can't feed you with a spoon all our lives. Get married and be someone else's shoulders' burden," her mother declared to her.

Ray was losing consciousness, the last word her mother said was echoing in her head. She had felt it. She had felt her mom's **burden**. She knew exactly what she had to do the next day before fading into the bliss of the unknown, the unconscious. Ray had fainted.

Chapter 8

BREAK-FREE

The next morning, her resolve from last night had kicked into her consciousness as soon as she took her first aware breath of the day, before she even opened her eyes. Ray could tell the time of the day, judging by the gleam coming from the green stained-glass window.

It must be close to 9 o' clock.

She noticed that her father had gone for work and not a sound was to be heard in the house. Her mother must have slept again habitually, after he left. Nobody had come in to check up on her as she had expected.

It was time. Ray immediately stood up, her head spun, her stomach growled next but she gathered herself and started to pack her bag. She wasn't worried about making any noise because not just that her mother was deep in her slumber, she wouldn't care even if she heard anything.

Ray was done with the packing but still had a morning face which was adorned by her swollen eyelids. She continued looking into the mirror only to apply a little lip-balm over her lips. She made a messy bun and put on her old square sunglasses. Changed into that one jeans that always worked. She looked at herself, one last time. Wiped that one savage tear from her face and smiled as bright as she could with the seventeen muscles at her disposal.

"It takes forty-three to frown," she wondered. Ray suddenly remembered to keep her medication just in case and picked up her hefty rucksack quite easily, for it was only her heart that felt real and heavy at the moment. Everything else was a fuzz. She slung the bag around her arms and reached the main door. It opened smoothly. Taking her time, she pushed it back into its place.

Now she was out, with nowhere to go. Her feet won't stop. They paced as fast as they could. She had left, she had run away.

Chapter 9

WATERS OF MEMORY

"Hey Sans," Ray said in an urgent voice without waiting for the other side to speak first on the phone.

"O hi girl... everything alright? You're calling at quite an odd time," Sanya said sympathetically.

"I was just wondering if I could come and meet you?" She was about to ask if she could live with her for a couple of days until she finds a room and a job.

"Yes, you can girl, but what's happened? Did your parents... say anything to you? Again?"

"Yeah they did. When do they not?"

"You seem really down. Okay, don't worry, come here and we'll have a good time together okay?"

"Yep, I'll see you. Bye."

"Bye."

"Hey Sans!"

"Yeah Ray?"

"You're the best you know. Love you."

"Aww... I love you too, bestie."

Ray was now sitting in the cab, looking out of the window. Suddenly, she looked at the glass, at her reflection; a resting bitch face and soon she dropped into the deep old waters of her memory...

It had happened way too often all through her life courtesy of her resting bitch face that people would randomly and abruptly ask her if she was okay. Ray would get nonplussed and delightfully nettled with their concern because—

One, yes she wasn't feeling okay and someone had noticed and

two, she could not go on and just give them the chronicles of her melancholic life in which she struggled to find a single happy moment.

Ray always had to convince them by giving a silly excuse like— she didn't sleep properly or something of the sort— "I had a little fight with my best friend." Even these lies seemed so real and nontheatrical because after all, she wasn't lying. She was only reporting on that fight that she had had with her best friend from kindergarten.

Ray shook it off and tried to look at the brighter side of the things for a moment. She opened up her wallet and there they were, the seven thousand rupees that she had won as a runner-up for her entrepreneurial idea in an intercollegiate event.

A smile suddenly streamed on her face and eased her aching chest. She remembered how awestruck she was in that moment and could barely make it to the stage with her wobbly mind and knees.

I didn't know back then that I was so good,

she heard in her mind.

I'm always going to stand up for myself.

A new air was breathed into her body. It revitalized her whole perception. Her heart warmed. Tears could not debut this time. She was born again from the ashes.

***

No! We're not doing this again.

Ray pulled her immersing self from the bittersweet, never changing, never moving lake of the past. The lake which changes only with the observer's judgement. When one looks down at it, it could reflect back a lesson or guilt; karma or a heart's wish. She tossed her blanket aside and sat up.

"I'm supposed to be sleeping, man..." She rubbed her eye peevishly. Ray sauntered to the mirror and there she was with her hair glamorously messed up and eyes beaming.

How can someone be so messed up from the inside and look perfectly fine on the outside? I mean, more than fine actually,

she wondered.

I'm good on the inside too, I'm still learning.

Ray decided she was not going to use her phone and was not even going to stay in the room either. So she slipped into her flip-flops, turned the lights off (always remember to turn the lights off) and locked the room.

Ray could feel a melodious touch of wind on her face as she went up the stairs. She almost jumped out after the last step and walked into her share of moonlight for the night.

Ray looked up and there it was, the waxing gibbous surrounded by two big, twisted clouds; one lit and another dark. They were closing in on the moon as if being sucked into a worm hole. It seemed as if they were to become the yin and yang.

Play of the elements.

She lied down on the ground to watch and seep in the everyday miracle, the moon, in front of her.

Chapter 10

DATED ENTRIES

The next day, after having sprouts and coconut water for breakfast, she opened that one sacred chamber in her cupboard which had a carton full of her aged stuff, dear to her heart.

Memoirs, old journals, forgotten novels and unforgettable goodies which were gifted to her. Inside of that box, she had the answers to her forever-questioning childlike mind and chronicles of the battles that she had won but forgotten somehow. She picked up that drabby, yellow, hardback diary which was gazing at her like an old crinkled Japanese lady watching the evening amblers, with her eyes tired, frozen in eternity; both the hands on her walking stick as she sat on the veranda waiting and who was upset because nobody visited her often.

Ray opened the pages carefully and to her delight, found a rap song that she had written, well, out of frustration because of the incessant bullying by the villainy college mean girls,

"Don't wanna be an impostor,

Don't wanna be festooned,

Cuz I'm hell real,

Cuz I'm hell real.

And yeah, I'll put my bid forward,

And don't need your validation,

Anymore, cuz I'm one of the smugs.

And you gave that shitty contempt look,

Like you were scared?

I'm gonna put you off the hook,

And your anecdotal murmuring,

Don't give a funny shit about them.

Baby, I was born unstoppable,

Was born with that struggle in me.

And I know now that pain is the flip side of remedy,

I won't repeat what you did to me,

Cuz I'm way smarter.

And you helped me achieve that too,

So thank you, so thank you,

Screw you."

They became friends later on.

She flipped some more pages from the back and found the page where, for the first time, she had written about her downcast comportment, the brain fog that never settled and the conundrum of attitudes towards her when she herself didn't know what was going on with her.

She took a cursory glance at it—

"Never thought that I'll be doing this but at this time, I see no other way and I've tried everything else. So I thought I'd give it a try and write about myself... I just don't understand myself. Whatever I try to do, never works. But I really need help or else I'll never try anything new in my life. I don't know what is wrong. I just want to die. I don't want to live."

Ray smiled at her younger self like a mother.

Only if that little girl had known that she was still going to be alive for years to come. And in all those years, she had become the school head girl, college pageant queen and was now working for one of the biggest companies in its field.

"Not bad for a person once contemplating suicide," she complimented and patted herself.

Her external confidence had definitely grown through the years and that made it all the more confusing because she still felt like shit inside. The only development she ever saw in her inner world was that she did not cry as often.

Improvement is improvement.

Ray was in a lifted frame of mind.

Flipped some more pages and she found the proofs of Pythagoras Theorem that she had found using random numbers two years before it was a thing in math class.

You go kiddo!

She was astonished at her own brilliance.

Chapter 11

LOVE LETTERS

Ray put the diary aside and rummaged through the box for anything that was unremembered that she could find next. One little box stuck out more than anything. It had in it, an abounding pile of love letters from admirers, who she never replied to because—

One, she was always too overwhelmed with the attention she got. She was perplexed about how could anyone be so obsessed with someone that they forget how to breathe at the sight of them, or they can't eat or sleep for days because their face haunts them?

What seemed to them like an unrequited love, seemed more like an uninvited obsession to her.

Two, she had never seen an ounce of attention from the same guys in real life. Nobody looked interested in her **that way**. They all looked like every other guy around her. So naturally, they seemed like cowards to her already.

"Stalker alert!" she blurted out in a mechanized hypo-nasal voice.

And three, if any guy had ever made an offer to her either online or in person, she never accepted because she didn't have eyes for anyone but Neil.

Ray travelled to that sweet past...

Just outside the cafeteria, he would stand amongst his gang like an alpha.

*Like an alpha? He **was** the alpha undoubtedly. But he wasn't too smug about it. Never.*

Just a few feet away from his circle, stood one more group of girlies in high heels, with perfect bodies, high ponytails and impeccable makeup. They always seemed to chortle and talk in a higher-than-normal pitch.

Ray searched for Neil from afar and found contentment at the sight of him. She immediately looked away as she started moving towards the cafeteria.

Ray would always have lunch with the quiet and modest Bhakti. She was slender, around five-seven with a pinkish complexion and soft features. Always had an impassive look on her face. She always had her hair braided without any finishing touch.

Bhakti was the dedicated, hardworking and studious one, always helped Ray with her assignments, all the time. Ray liked her for that and also because she did not talk about guys and fads all the time. On the other hand, Bhakti was always and only interested in studies. She had even brought her notebook to the cafeteria to munch on her freshly made notes. Bhakti wasted no time and Ray respected that.

As they approached the entrance, Ray felt her heart beating erratically; breathing deep, every step was suddenly heavier as she passed beside Neil. She felt his eyes on her and her cheeks burned. As usual, Ray and Bhakti sat on the corner table with their usual muffins and milkshake.

Ray started eating immediately. She was always hungry while Bhakti nibbled, lost in revising proof of the Fundamental Theorem of Calculus.

Every now and then, Ray would try to look outside to catch Neil's glimpse or listened intently to hear his virile, soft, deep and soothing voice that pierced through everyone else's noise. He did not talk much, only made a remark here and there. Ray did not know why but it felt like he wasn't really paying attention to the mocking conversation about the viral girl who had sung a pesky rap song in her peskier voice. It went something like this—

"Bow down to me,

I'm your queen.

Brush your teeth,

before you come to me."

Ray didn't want to think about the remainder of it.

"She's hot though," said one himbo from the group.

Suddenly, they all started to walk into the cafeteria and Ray started to eat pretentiously. She spotted Neil spotting her and somehow, none of them looked away. He walked past her and finally, the spell broke. He sat on the table beside hers. After a few seconds came in the girlies following them and she felt her goosebumps settle finally.

Chapter 12

AGAINST GRAVITY

I wasn't moving, wasn't going forward.

So I set fire to the forest of Past.

The flames reached for me,

And now,

I run.

Ray smiled heartily to herself. She was in her room again and still smiling.

"Maybe I shouldn't dwell on the past so much. I still have a lot left to do."

Even the thought of Neil used to fill her with so much energy. The power-of-love type of energy.

I can't keep doing this.

A thought of rebellion declared.

It's been a good long while of me working here but let's face it, it's not somewhere I can be all my life. I only happened to stumble here. But I have to leave someday, for something more. I'm more than just someone who goes to office everyday only to come back tired. I'm more than just appreciation and accolades. I can do better than this.

Yes, you are better than this.

She sighed in relief as if a hurricane had been calmed down to become the wise sea again. Her eyes blinked, several times and she removed her attention from her mind to the box. She was looking for something else in that—a rusted, mini chocolate box.

"Oh! there it is."

She picked it up, swiped the dust from its lid gently with three fingers.

"It has to be in here."

It was something that she would play with all the time in her school days and even years later. It used to sit on her desk all day, everyday, as it watched the birds fly through the window while she studied.

She pressed upon the lid and lifted it up. There it was. The Alphapeak-77. Well, just a miniature model that she had made herself with clay and cardboard. It was coarse on the surface and its wings had dwindled a bit on the tips. But recreating a miniature model of the 50 million dollar aircraft that pushed on earth with a 333,786 kilogram force, with her own two hands was the only way that she could keep the Roc of an aircraft next to herself.

Ray remembered how the plane used to look so big when she looked at it from her table's surface. She would imagine herself in a helmet and a pilot's suit, steering the beast at hyper-sonic speeds and doing somersaults above 10,000 ft. from the sea level.

All alone with the clouds and the sun. Who knows, she might see a UFO or something. And maybe someday, she could actually go into the outer space and look at mother earth's might from an alien's perspective.

Oh to fall foerever in zero gravity.

And why only stop there? Visit every planet in the solar system; even just to get a good look from their orbits and then go beyond the solar system, the galaxy even.

Travel through a wormhole if possible. But never was she going to stop unless she had seen the very end of the universe and back. Maybe, she could finally figure out God after seeing all of that. Or find out what he must be thinking. And then create a universe of her own and be the God herself. Was there anything cooler?

Chapter 13

A DOPE DAWNING

Ray had gotten so caught up in the whirlwind of getting away from home, supporting herself and trying to outrun her glum past, that she had totally forgotten that she still had a future nonetheless. She took the plane and placed it on her table and put the box back into its sacred chest only to be discovered again. Perhaps later on, sometime.

"The Air Force Admission Test is held in August every year. That's four months from now," she calculated.

"That's not a lot of time but I can try again in February after gaining some experience."

Are you counting on the fact that you're going to fail? That's a very lazy thought honestly,

a thought in her head teased. A thought teasing another thought.

It's not lazy. It's called plan B.

She moved her chin to the left and pursed her lips in contemplation.

You know what? Maybe you're right. I can't count on just 'trying' on my first attempt. That defeats the purpose of it all if I'm starting out with defeat in my head.

"So, the narrative goes something like this: we're doing this in the very first attempt no matter what anyone says."

That's more like it.

Ray didn't care that she would have to wake up an hour earlier to run in the morning and sleep an hour later after studying.

At least I'm going to have a schedule in place. Much needed.

At this point, she just wanted to give it all.

Even if—

She hesitated to even think.

*Even if I feel like crying or feel hollow inside or feel like it's doomsday. Maybe it's time to start taking the pills again. I'm going to get better. **I have to**. After all the discipline and focus, I **will** get better by the time. I'm through.*

She breathed out with conviction in her eyes.

"Okay now don't get too motivated, we have to sleep too," she reminded herself immediately.

She always had a hard time relaxing so it was better to take her own advice if she was to sleep at all and that too according to the schedule. But before that—

"Clothes decided for the next day? Check.

Old sports shoes out? Check.

Alarm clock? Check."

Everything was ready. Monday didn't look so blue anymore. She got cozied up in the bed and focused on her breath. Luckily, her mind was at ease that day and she fell asleep.

Cheers to a goodnight's sleep.

Chapter 14

PROPHETIC

'I'll take care of it,' she heard from behind her. Something had moved from inside of her and disappeared into the streamline of future. She looked back at it and it looked back at her. She saw none but herself smiling the sweetest smile.

"Even the sky is not the limit. Ha-ha. See? I told you." Ray looked down from her cockpit while flying closer and closer to the sun. She might run into it anytime now.

"I can see heaven from here," she shouted at two little blurry people standing on the ground who were looking back at her. How peculiar that the heat was not able to touch her even though it clearly showed on the thermocouple. Must be the material of the jet. And also, how the sky was still blue?

"We were wrong about you dear, come back to us," her mom said with teary eyes. Wait! They could hear her?

Ray listened and looked at her dad who was smiling, teared up. He didn't say anything but he was definitely proud to see her daughter fly.

She was now looking at the sun. Eye to eye. Filled with joy and stories to tell later on, she steered the aircraft back to earth.

"The stars for tomorrow," she shouted triumphantly. Wait, she was coming down too fast, out of control. The aircraft had caught fire and suddenly it was a blue, lit up meteorite against the dark starry background. Her whole universe was spinning like an endless ball and she was stuck inside.

"I can't crash," she said to herself as she approached earth and **IMPACT!**

She was lying there on the soft grass as if it had been forever.

"You look good today," said Mohit.

She looked at him and got drawn to his shoes. "New shoes today?" Ray wondered how he got there. "Wait. What the heck?"

A soft masterly piano piece starts to play in the background. It was her alarm.

Ray opened her eyes and felt great. She smiled at the feeling. Then it downloaded in her awareness—

Got to go for a run...

The morning haze had not lifted yet outside and it seemed as if the trees were blanketed in it. The first light had just arrived. She looked up at the sky, remembering her travel to beyond its limits. And started to run with a smirk on her face and eyes leering at the prospects of the rest of her life.

Ray reached the park which was just a street away from her room. It was packed, mostly with the elderly who used to practice yoga in groups. A few lads were jogging. There was also this person in seclusion who was the type to perform the toughest of the yoga poses. She recognized the pose he was making; hand stand scorpion. And he performed them without any discomfort or embarrassment.

Impressive, I should try to do that too. But on the bed.

She laughed at the **inside joke.**

Okay, now time to run.

She ran as fast as she could for two minutes and then halted out of breath. Ray breathed heavily from her mouth and put hands on her hips. And when her breath steadied, she went for it again. Lasted for only a minute at the most this time. She could feel her cheeks burning and her whole body bathed in sweat. Ray just wanted to get out of her hoodie right away but hesitated in front of all those people.

Okay... let's just walk then and cool off.

Ray looked at her watch. An hour had passed. She did some last few stretches and ran to hit the shower as soon as possible.

"Hey beautiful!" She blew herself a kiss in the mirror and got into her car.

"We've got to eat better too..."

Ray always addressed herself in plural because she wasn't just talking to her conscious self but also to the subconscious self **and** her body. Yeah, she read too many books on spirituality and psychology.

***

Ray reached office and parked her car. She was feeling lighter today contrary to bygone days so she leapt up the stairs, two at once.

"Woo, miss, watch where you're going."

She recognized the voice and laughed.

"Hi Mohit."

"Hi, you look good today."

Something moved inside her head. Has she not heard that before? Déjà vu hit her. She looked at Mohit's feet intuitively.

"New shoes today?" she said with her eyebrows raised.

The bright yellow colour was not the reason of her astonishment at all but to him, it looked so.

"Glad you like them."

"Yeah, they go with the khaki trousers too." She added to be more believable.

Ray was keeping up with the office schedule with her stomach growling every now and then.

More food and better food from now on.

She finished with her day somehow. Ray reached her room and ate dinner without changing. After finishing her meal she quickly changed into her pajamas and immediately, felt her eyes going heavy and her body craving the bed.

"Yeah sure, now I feel all sleepy. Great! I wonder if I should throw all the pills away…" she yawned.

"… and continue with this schedule."

That reminded her of something. Ray took out the pills, eight bister packs from her bag and singled out the sleeping pills and put them aside. She popped one from each of the remaining seven and placed some books on the table– English, Reasoning and Quantitative Aptitude. Ray started with Reasoning but her eyes went out of focus. She tried again, same thing happened. Then she forced a thought in her drowsy head.

Just one problem, each book.

Some energy flowed back in her and she solved the problems one by one. Happy about accomplishing her goal, she turned the lights off without losing a second and fell asleep in no time. With a beautiful smile of satisfaction on her face.

Chapter 15

CRASH-DOWN

Another day, she woke up, ran, ate, drove, worked, drove back, ate, studied, slept and repeated the next day.

"You seem really quiet these days," said Mohit and Ray was dehypnotized. She was busy thinking of the next thing to do. She was always thinking of the next thing to do.

"Am I? Didn't notice."

"Also, you look thinner. Are you on a diet or something?" Mohit made a puffy face and punched her shoulder lightly.

"Me on a diet? Never. It's just that I jog everyday in the morning." She was proud.

"Brave of you to wake up so early, I could never. I get back from here, make dinner with my roomies and drink a little, *because of them.* Then we all drift off."

Neither did Ray like to drink nor did she like the people who did but she was careful enough to never come across as judgmental.

"Yeah, peer pressure. I've never drunk in my life... Tasted it once but didn't feel like I was into it. Not even planning to." She raised one hand and drew away from Mohit instinctively and playfully.

Margosa leaves dipped in honey.

But Mohit never seemed to mind her bittersweet.

***

Two weeks went by peacefully, all according to her plan and conviction but then, it happened again.

"Hey Mohit," she said in a nosy voice that is usually there after crying.

"Hey Ray, good morning! Good Lord, you're calling now? It's almost office time. Are you getting late? Why do you sound sick?"

"Yeah... I'm not feeling well today. So I guess I won't be coming to work," she said guiltily.

"But what about the drill today? I hope you remember that all the top executives will be visiting today and none of us is expected to be AWOL."

Ray felt even worse than before and it made it all the way harder to speak. She almost choked with the pain in her being.

"Hello? Are you there? Ray?"

"Yeah, yeah I'm here," she said catching her breath instantly. "I don't know Mohit. How will I make it? I really can't even move from the bed."

"But what happened to you?"

A series of events went through her head starting right from the moment when she opened her eyes in the morning, how she has been feeling ghostly even after having her usual healthy breakfast and listening to her favorite songs. It had seemed like a struggle to even stand without feeling dizzy and then she dropped on her bed exhausted. In the morning!

"Ray?"

"I don't know, my whole body is aching and I feel dizzy," she half-lied. She did that a lot to avoid explanations.

"Okay then, you have rest and drop an e-mail to the coordinator when I tell you so. I'll talk to him."

"No you don't have to, I mean I'll handle it tomorrow, whatever happens."

"You don't think that I can help you? You're one of the best here. He will listen."

"Because you're the best."

"Not to brag, but the friendship between him and I goes beyond the office hours. So you don't worry."

"Okay then, if you say so."

"Now take care. See you tomorrow?"

"Yeah I don't know how to thank you. But, thank you."

"That's insulting."

Ray giggled weakly, "Okay then mention not?"

"Er... whatever. I'm getting late now. See you later."

"Okay. Good day."

"Take care."

"Sure," she said, not knowing what she had already not been doing to make sure she were okay. What else did she need to do?

Ray put the phone aside and closed her eyes but there was no escaping the pain. She opened her eyes to focus, involuntarily, on the bright sunlight outside her window and the leaves of trees flapping gently. Ray could hear a bird chirp and jump from one branch to another. She decided to focus on it, a red vented bulbul. It seemed that her chest and throat pinched every time it fluttered.

Ray hid her face instinctively in the mattress.

How can this be? Now an innocent bird is hurting me too? What's wrong with me? Maybe I should take the sleeping pill.

It's not good to overdose on those,

A thought echoed in her empty and howling head.

Fine. I'll just try and meditate lying down here.

She found her favorite guided meditation and played it. The unusually soothing voice of the narrator now seemed like pins being poked in her ears. She grew irritated and threw the headphones aside. Ray put her head in her hands.

God help me!

And for once, it all went quiet. Just a silent silence. No thoughts, no sobs. She could breathe for once and she lay there without moving for a couple of minutes. "Thank you..."

Chapter 16

THE FIRST TEXT

Ray was sitting there with a pencil between her teeth, trying to understand the Interference of Light.

Her phone beeped.

Who could be texting at this hour?

She opened her messenger and could not believe what her eyes were seeing. Her eyes doubled and eyebrows hit the ceiling. The pencil had dropped on the floor. She blinked several times to double-check what she was witnessing. She felt her cheeks burn. She caught herself looking in the mirror suddenly, adjusting her hair and wiping the oil around her nose even though there was no one else to look at her in her single college hostel room. Ray facepalmed upon realizing that.

Her feet didn't know where the earth was and she jumped and flew and stopped and spun around; totally out of touch with reality.

Could it really be Neil?!

No way... it must be something else that he's texting because of. Notes?

Yeah... I'm pretty smart but I thought he was better at studies than me. Maybe he misidentified me for another person.

"Girl, okay whatever it is, let's find out. It'll be rude to not reply."

She picked up her phone and texted him a simple but hefty, "Hi."

There was an instant reply.

Neil: Hi, I hope I didn't disturb you.

Ray: No, not at all. I'm only surprised.

Neil: Why?

Ray: Because we've never talked before.

Neil: So you don't talk to strangers?

Ray: No, I didn't mean it that way. I mean we've never talked in class.

Neil: Well I guess, we're talking now.

She felt her cheeks fill.

Ray: Well, um... did you need anything? Notes or something?

Neil: Actually no, none of that.

She was relieved.

Ray: So..?

Neil: So I just want to get to know you more.

She was flattered. But she wasn't sure if there was anything special to know about her.

Ray: I don't think there's anything special about me to know.

Neil: I do.

Was it really happening? Everything had stopped existing but the two.

Ray: I don't know why you think so.

Neil: Not just me, there are many who think so.

Ray: Well... I don't care about everyone. She slipped and facepalmed again.

Neil: Then who do you care about?

Ray: I don't know, someone that I know. Maybe.

Neil: I would like to know more about you. Do you think the same about me?

Ray: Yes.

She said spell bound.

Neil: ☺

Ray: ☺

***

She put her phone aside. The old forgotten texts were making her feel weepy. But Neil was still hovering in her head.

It's been ages since I talked to him... But I guess it's better that way. Guess I'm going to stalk him online!

No, I have better things to do.

"But I don't want to study either..." she whined.

"Damn it! I need to feel okay for a breather."

Ray went through some business and fashion magazines for pure entertainment purposes.

She read about the next youngest entrepreneur who was on the cover with his arms crossed and with a big smile, too big for the camera even. Must be the happiness of being featured in one of the biggest magazines, or perhaps, it's the three-hundred million dollar company that he owned.

She looked at him, analyzed him for a moment, then quickly jumped through the pages.

Ray read about an illiterate old lady accompanied by eight other widows who had been able to start their very own popular, hut-styled and solar-powered restaurant for anyone who passed by their village.

Next, she read an exclusive interview of the Miss Universe and the Best Male Debutant in Bullywood.

A bunch of how to's too:

How to make your pony higher?

How to make your makeup last?

How to choose the best salad for yourself according to your zodiac?

How to woo the man of your dreams?

How to select the right crystals for your chakra healing?!

Ray was exhausted.

"How can I read so much and still feel like I didn't read anything actually. Ugh."

She tossed the glazy magazines aside and thought of posting a picture of herself in a high pony. 333 likes. Comments turned off. She was happy.

Chapter 17

PRE D-DAY

Should I call mom and tell her?

No. I'll tell her after the exam.

The D-Day was the next day only. Neither did Ray have high hopes nor a fear of failure. She was unusually calm too.

I've done everything and now it's just one more day and then it'll all be done. It'll all be good.

She reassured herself.

Ray checked all the requirements again— id proof, admit card, photographs, pen, change and notes.

"No, not notes. I'll revise only until just before leaving. Nothing after that."

She was unusually level-headed too.

Ray arranged her clothes and the articles neatly on the table and opened her notes. She held them in her lap and read from them in her mind loudly. Ray found that she had remembered most of it. She had only been able to really prepare the 70% of the syllabus. For the rest, she counted on her studying done in college.

"I think it's enough now. If I get too stressed, I won't be able to sleep."

She parted from the notes and lied down. For a second, she thought of calling Sanya.

No. Leave it. I'll talk to her tomorrow. Can't afford to talk about anything else and lose my focus.

She lied down and visualized the exam hall, the exam paper, how she would write and solve effortlessly and how she'd come out smiling and victorious. Ray smiled with the vision.

Then, something occurred to her.

How about I write the formulae on my thighs. I'll be wearing jeans so nobody's going to know and I can go through them in the washroom.

She smiled wickedly.

"Ah, I'll decide tomorrow if I'm going to do it or not."

She lied down and closed her eyes. Ray wanted to pray and didn't want to. But then she did.

God, I trust you. I know, only the best will happen. Thank you. Love you.

Ray closed her eyes and waited for the sweet sleep to come. She had gone to bed an hour earlier so she could really relax. But instead, came visions of her future prospects.

She saw herself in the pilot uniform with aviators on.

She also saw the smile on her parents' faces and saw them embracing her. Even her dad did!

She saw Neil looking dumbfounded at her.

She saw Sanya drowning her in her huge arms and she saw Mohit becoming sad because she was not going to be in the office anymore.

"Don't worry, we'll stay in touch," she would say to him.

"Okay, now let's sleep."

Ray focused completely on her breathing. One hour passed, she was still very much awake and her body would twist and turn in the bed.

It wasn't my usual time so perhaps I can sleep now.

Another hour passed and Ray felt that her eyes were dry. No sign of sleep. She kept patient and kept on trying to focus on her breath.

Great! Now I can't sleep even after taking care of everything.

No, don't get discouraged Ray, we'll sleep.

She felt her eyes go limp and her chest relaxed. But suddenly came the image of an exam hall and her body became active and attentive again in a bolt.

Every time, she felt a little hope of sleeping, one fit or the other of the future would startle her. Sometimes, she saw sticky and painful images of the past and it would tinge her.

Ray found herself in a constant war where all the bad bullets of memory and fireballs of fear of the future were being shot at her. She felt alone. Just before she was about to cry, she stopped herself and sat up on the bed.

I think I should take the pill.

But what if I over sleep? There's a good chance of that happening.

I don't care, I need to sleep.

She had become irritated.

Okay, I'm going to take only half of it,

she came to the conclusion. She picked up her phone and checked if the alarm volume was high enough. It was. She jumped out from her bed, popped the pill and lay down giving out a huge sigh. Ray felt sleep descending on her and she could let it go at last.

Chapter 18

D-DAY

Her eyes creaked open. Ray felt stress in her under eyes and a strange strain in her head. She looked out of the window, the sun was not out yet. There was no ounce of light outside. She picked up her phone unwillingly and looked at the time and her chest drew back. It had been only two hours since she fell asleep!

Great!

Now Ray had only two hours left to sleep and after that she would have to revise her notes and get ready. She had hoped to sleep for a good time before the exam. And now, that wasn't possible anymore. The disappointment made her blood run awake and she sat up.

No. I have to go back to sleep.

She popped the other half of the pill and drifted off.

Her alarm rang only once and she was as awake as an eagle. Ray immediately snatched her notes from the table and went through each and every line with unwavering focus and attention. Her tongue was reciting the formulae as fast as her brain read them. In one perfect focused sweep, she finished reading the notes in forty-five minutes.

Now was the time to put them aside and never look back at them. Ray had her usual breakfast and fought her drowsiness with a cold shower it was going to stay even after that though. She had not the time to pay attention to it. Ray looked at herself in the mirror, her eyes were blood shot and her skin looked paler.

"I look quite sexy like this."

***

Ray reached the hall five minutes earlier than the allotted time and got seated. Now was the time to revisit her vision that she had created the last night—of her writing and solving the paper effortlessly.

The bell rang and she jumped in.

Chapter 19

GOOD LUCK

Ray was sitting at her desk as usual and she saw Viyona coming in. She was going from one desk to another in order to check if things were going well with the new software update. Ray tried to focus on her work but could not because she knew that Viyona will be there in a minute and she will surely ask about the—

"Hello Rayveena, everything working fine with the new software?"

"Hi Viyona, yes everything is good."

"And how did your exam go?" She stood comfortably with one hand on her desk and the other in her pocket.

"It was okay."

"Just... okay?" Viyona hated okay, everyone knew that.

"Yeah... kind of." Ray lifted her nose and eyebrows as she kept analyzing every micromovement of Viyona's face.

"Aww, I don't want you to leave us you know?"

Ray kept looking at Viyona and waited for her to continue.

"But I'll be the happiest if you get through. Good luck," she said charmingly.

Ray blinked sweetly and said, "Thank you." Ray didn't actually think that her exam was just okay. She just did not want to count the chickens before they even hatched.

"...So when will your result be out miss?" Ray jumped inside her mind by the mention. She was still lost in her conversation with Viyona, balancing every word of hers against her own.

"Oh, going by the curve, it takes around 40-45 days," she said to Mohit.

"That's great! So soon, you'll be leaving us."

Ray tried to act surprised narrowing her eyes and opening her mouth as if she were to say something. She loved to let her face do the talking, when she really wanted to.

Then she carried on, "Well, that's not certain you know. There's no way to know that. I didn't even have enough time in my hands. You know. So..."

"You're very bad at pretending," he laughed to himself.

"Well, I wasn't... I really don't know how it will turn out."

"You'll be through for sure. I know that. Good luck!"

"Thanks."

Chapter 20

ALLEVIATION

Ray tried her password one more time, but the webpage was not loading.

"Hey, what happened?" Sanya enquired on the phone. She was chewing something.

"It's not... responding."

"Try one more time."

"Yeah."

She entered her email and password one more time and the webpage loaded. For a moment, she froze. Ray was staring at the laptop screen but with blurry eyes. Not because of any ailment but because she was not focusing deliberately.

"Hey Sans, it's showing."

"Finally... what's it say?"

"I haven't looked. Look, I'm sending you the screenshot, you tell me what it says."

"Oh come on, don't be afraid now. You took pains for this test and now you don't even want to look?" Sanya tried to talk some sense into her.

"Yeah, right." She opened her eyes one by one that she had closed whilst replying to Sanya. The screen got less and less blurry. Her narrowed eyes got drawn towards the bottom of the page.

Cut off marks: 150

Your score : 159

"What? Not even 160?" Ray almost shouted.

Congratulations! You are qualified for the next stage of testing.

Sanya spit out her gum and jumped to her rescue. "What? It's okay girl don't fret, you can take the next one. Right?"

"It says you're qualified for the next stage of testing," Ray said weakly.

"Oh thank God... What? That means you're through?"

"Um... yes. Sans."

"Party partee parteeeeh!"

Finally, Ray smiled. "Yeah for sure. But only me and you."

"Oh I knew it, you can never fail. You're the best. Did you tell your mom?"

"Well, I haven't talked to her."

"Since..?"

"In a long while."

"Oh come on, you've got to tell them. They'll be surprised."

"Yeah... okay I will," Ray said, convinced.

"Girl, my phone's about to die. I'll call you and we'll decide when and where to celebrate."

"Yeah sure," Ray said cheerfully.

"Congratulations again. I love you."

"Love you. Bye."

Ray looked at the screen once again.

It's happened!

She smiled like diamonds.

"I didn't think I could, yet it's here." A little tear slipped from the corner of her eye and she did not stop it.

Memories of sleepless nights, of how tired she used to be after office hours, of her tears, of the dark hours she spent inside her cupboard, they all came out of somewhere and burst out of her.

Ray cried blatantly to acknowledge and celebrate those pains that she had not gotten the chance to attend to before. For she had bound herself to the schedule.

But it's only half the battle.

She wiped her tears and decided to celebrate the moment anyway. Even though Ray wanted to tell her parents about this only after she had cleared all the rounds, something in her, a child, still wanted her parents' approval and appreciation.

***

Ring... ring... Ring... ring... It went on and on. "Maybe I shouldn't—"

"Hello? Hello?" her mother picked up.

"Uh... hello?" Ray said weakly.

"Yah... I was just preparing food."

"I see."

"Hello?"

"I'm still here mom."

"Oh and how is your job? Are you still working there?"

"Yes."

"As you wish. Why would you listen to us anymore? Who are we to you anyway?"

"Where's my remote?" said another voice in the background, Ray's father's.

Ray cowered a little upon hearing the harshness in his tone.

"Just wait a minute. Will you? Yes, I'm coming! I'll have to go. I'll call you later."

"Okay no—" and the phone hung up. "problem…"

Chapter 21

FUTURE PLANS

"So, what are your future plans?"

"Mm?" Ray looked up while sipping her chocolate-shake.

"What do you mean? Future plans? Are you so ready to get married?"

Neil chuckled upon hearing that.

"That, we can do later on, but I'm talking about your future plans, your career."

"Oh." Ray looked down at the table and started to trace the circles on it, sitting in their favorite restaurant. "I haven't thought about it."

She did not because she had no particular attraction to the popular notion of a career, let alone the idea of a successful career. Ray had been told she had a lot of potential by many of her peers even by Neil but she had never felt it. Like a rose knows not its own beauty and fragrance but surely knows how to produce the velvety petals, the ivory-white hue and the guards up all around it.

She just did not know what exactly she wanted to do. And what she wanted to gain from it.

"There must be something that you've thought of doing after finishing college. Like, you are so good at public speaking, you could easily get into sales and marketing or you could become a lecturer and if you want, you could go for higher studies. You're one of the smartest persons I know." Neil suggested. He had an out-and-out belief in her abilities.

She thought of the other things that she was really good at—

Dancing, making art, making up stories, acting, persuading people (when she needed to), seeing a plan through to its execution, gardening—

"Say something."

She looked up at him and gulped. "Yeah, I don't think my parents will be too happy about the higher studies thing."

"So which one would you prefer out of the ones I just told you? Your parents won't be supportive but I will be for sure, but you have to choose a path for yourself first."

"I know, you're always there for me." She reached out for his hand and he held her hand in both of his.

"Of course, just think about what I said."

"Sure, what about you?"

His eyes gleamed instantly. "About me? Well... I'm preparing for an interview with Vel-E."

"That's great..." Ray said with an air of pride.

"Yeah! I've already taken the written test and it was, honestly, very easy." His eyes were gleaming stars.

"I'm sure."

"Yeah, so if I get through, your Neil will be working for one of the biggest companies in the world."

Ray chuckled at the way he put it. There was nothing she wanted more than his happiness.

"Definitely," she said.

Neil continued, "And then after gaining enough experience, I'll surely move abroad."

"And then, you will find a new girlfriend there," Ray joked seriously and sipped from the cup.

"Mm, probably," Neil chuckled.

Ray gave him a death stare.

"You look hot like that."

She smiled, he smiled. And they both fell into the depth of each other's eyes.

Chapter 22

A GOOD PLACE TO EAT

Ray kept peering out at the street intently as she walked and twirled, directionless, in her black moto boots on the gravel outside of her room. She called Sanya again.

"How long?"

"I'm right around the corner."

"Okay." she heard the familiar horn and looked behind her. Sanya stopped the car with a drift and honked again. Ray quickly opened the car door and got inside the supermini.

"You look great!" Ray complimented.

Sanya fluttered her eyes a little and smiled. "Yeah it's a brand new top. A gift actually."

"Oh really... from whom?" Ray teased.

"Oh come on, no one that you're thinking of. Mom."

"Her choice is awesome. By the way, you look great in everything."

"You're cho chweet," Sanya chirped.

"I'm sorry, I couldn't bring my car and you had to ask your dad. My car is... well the steering wheel shakes and on top of that, the battery is dead. Guess it wasn't that great an idea to buy second hand. Don't know how and when I'll be able to get it repaired."

"Well you know, as they say, it's better to have second hand diamonds than to have none at all."

"Huh, are you serious? You think that's a diamond? Please. It's the cheapest bargain I've ever made. 60k for a car! I mean I probably have the cheapest car in my whole office. But I'm grateful that I have one... or had one."

"But anyway, how did you arrange for the money, you don't have to tell me, just curious," Sanya said looking straight ahead at the road.

"I had gotten 40k as my college refund and the rest, was supported by dad, I used to be very stubborn." She lied about the last part.

The rest had been supported by Neil and she did not want to talk about him because if she brought up his name, there will be endless questions and she did not want to deal with that. Not now. It was supposed to be a happy day.

Ray kept staring out at the familiar streets that she had once walked, hand-in-hand with Neil.

"So...? Where are we going sleeping beauty?"

"You tell me, we could go anywhere you like. I just want that we spend time together. That's more important," Ray said in one breath.

"But still, we could go somewhere different this time. I heard about a new place called Lotuslore. How about we go there and see how it is?"

"Okay."

The two pals went in and were mesmerized by the decor of the restaurant. It was everything the name suggested. There were big, five feet big, blue star-lotuses with softly glowing centers on each wall but one. The one lucky wall had a raised, gigantic looking masterpiece of Lord Krishna sitting lightly, with his eyes lost in eternal bliss and with a lotus on his forehead.

The lotus-eyed one,

clicked in her head. "Wow," escaped from her mouth.

"We will take a selfie with it later. For sure."

"Yes," said Ray with her eyes still lingering. She was not really prepared to encounter Krishna in a commercial setting.

Maybe the owner hasn't created this restaurant for money, but for his love for lotuses and Krishna,

she imagined.

The tables inside were designed and shaped resembling the lotus fruit but the surface was given a glossy finish. Despite that, the table's vision brought the trypophobia out of her and she had goosebumps whenever she found herself staring at them for too long.

Who ever thought that lotus fruit was somehow aesthetically appealing, is probably blind.

There was an intoxicating fragrance spilled all over the air. They looked farther and found the source of the aroma. It was a pond right in the center of the floor and it had about thirty frankly-scarlets.

"That's so beautiful," they both spoke together and laughed.

"Let's take that one," Sanya said pointing towards a table near the pond. They both sat there and Ray realized that the table finishing was actually sprinkled with glitter and that made it not so eerie anymore to look at.

"As they say, a little sparkle makes everything better," she said aloud and tapped on the table two times.

"Yes! That's right baby," Sanya agreed. She picked a card that was laying there on the table and squeaked, "Oh look, it's so pretty."

"What, show me."

It was a picture of a parrot-beak lotus. It said,

'Just like the parrot beak's fiery red colour,

something might set your senses on fire today...'

Awarded International flower of the year.

"Didn't know flowers had competitive exams too," Ray joked.

"Really, I really wonder what might stir... my soul today," Sanya said twirling her hair. "Or yours!"

"Er, excuse me mam."

"Yes, we'd like some water first please," said Sanya immediately.

"Yes mam definitely, but let me show you to another table. This one is reserved."

"Oh okay, no problem." Ray started to stand up expecting Sanya to do the same.

"Wait, there isn't even a sign on the table. You should have put it here. Is that how you treat your customers? I want you to pass on the message to your entire team. If the sign had been there we would've saved a lot of our time and yours too." Sanya gave him a piece of her mind in one breath.

"Yes mam, please do come with me. I'll show you to your table and bring soda for you both."

"Yes, we'd like that thank you," said Sanya triumphantly.

"Hey wait, do we have to—"

The waiter cut Ray mid-sentence, "No mam, it's on us for the inconvenience caused."

"Okay... good," Ray sighed and settled in the seat.

"Let's see who sits there," Sanya said, eyes peering.

"Sans... don't," Ray said with an adorable look and Sanya smiled.

"Let's order something." Ray opened the menu. "I'll eat Mexican salad and you?"

"I want to try this portobello mushroom burger and something to drink?" Sanya asked.

"Pomegranate and beet smoothie... What?" Ray caught Sanya giving her that I-don't-believe-you look.

"It's good for health Sans... you should order something like... ya! Grapefruit and rosemary mocktail."

"Fine, we are just getting started but after this, we're going to have a **real meal.** Understood?"

Ray chuckled, "Yeah sure if we have any pocket left."

A few moments later...

A tall guy walked in with a tall and super thin girl and they headed towards the reserved seat. No doubt, the guy looked expensive in a long black overcoat. He had a sharp verdi beard and an english moustache; definitely looked like someone in his mid-thirties. His black eyes were small and sharp and had a darkness around them, Ray observed.

"He looks kind of intense… like a detective. The only thing that he's missing is a hat," said Sanya.

"Maybe. The girl definitely looks like a model though. I think she's a model," Ray said, chewing, judging by her sleek ponytail and height of course.

"Yeah. Do you think they're a couple?" Sanya asked with a pained expression.

"Hardly, they look more businesslike."

They had spread some pictures on the table and were having a conversation inaudible to the girls.

Ray observed furthermore that the guy was laughing quite amazingly but it was kind of… sickly. The girl was definitely laughing pretentiously even though her whole body language said she was enjoying the conversation. Meanwhile, Sanya couldn't stop staring and gushing over the guy.

"Stop it, they'll notice Sans."

Five minutes later, the girl stood up, gave him a big smile and a hug and walked out too quickly. She might have cast a quick-look in the girls' direction.

The guy stood up after paying the bill.

"That's ridiculous," said Sanya through her teeth.

"What?"

"I think he's walking towards us."

"What? He must've noticed you staring," Ray whispered angrily.

"O my god Ray, he's definitely coming here."

Chapter 23

A PROFFER

"Hello ladies, I didn't mean to interrupt but I couldn't help but notice the two lovelies sitting here," he said lovelies looking at Sanya who was already looking at him with eyes wide open.

"I'm Dev, a photographer. I work for a magazine called GlamClaim. Nice to meet you." He gently shook hands with both of them.

"Please, have a seat," Ray forced out.

"No thanks. I have to go and meet a client of mine. I found you guys quite fascinating and I wonder if you'd like to model for me."

Ray rolled her eyes and Sanya made a face towards her.

"Thank you very much, we shall need time to think about it," Sanya said and Ray kicked her foot under the table.

"Take all the time you need, here's my card. Contact me anytime, 24/7. Nice meeting you again." He gave a look which was surely directed at Ray.

"Yes," was all she could say. Her cheeks went red unwillingly.

And he left in his large SUV.

"It's Dev, the photographer! That was him," Sanya shouted silently.

"Who? I've never heard of him and that magazine of his."

"How could you ever. You never spend time out of your books and work. He's worked with stars like Priyanjali and Deepshikha."

"Really?!"

"Yes. I'm telling you."

"But if he's such a celebrity, why would he walk up to us complete strangers?"

"Didn't you listen? Because he wants us to model for him."

"I don't want to do any modelling and neither do you Sans."

"Oh come on, you should visit his website and maybe it'll change your mind and then we could both go to his studio."

"Let's focus on the food for now. Okay?"

"Okay!" Sanya squeaked.

The sky was being extra creative in the evening. Ray looked outside and up out of the window. It was grey, then golden in the middle and then blue on her right. The sun seemed like it had already drifted off to a great dream, blanketed in a hazy halo. In fact, the whole sky seemed to be in a haze, as though drunk. Dark clouds with a lighter streak in between had gathered right above the sun and it looked gothic as if hiding a dark secret, desperate to come out into the light.

Right above her, where the clouds had not arrived yet, was an enchanting golden wash spread. And strangely enough, to the east, were clouds like cotton balls, dark and light, about to fall down on the earth. The wind, was like waves sometimes cold and sometimes warm. It touched her face as the car seemed to be drifting towards nothing.

Aren't we all like that? All this hurry to go where? It's all here. In the moment,

she felt. Ray had become one with the magic, lost herself in it. "So beautiful," she whispered to herself.

If there were no one around, she would have danced with the wind at the four-way junction.

"Is it legit?"

The spell was broken. Sanya was waiting for her to answer and at last, Ray came back to her senses.

"Legit? Oh yeah. I looked it up. He seems legit to me. There are pictures with the stars on his website. It says he's looking for models for a body positivity shoot."

"See? I told you. Here we are..." And Sanya stopped the car.

"I had a great time Sans, always do with you." And they hugged each other goodbye.

Chapter 24

A LONE WOLF

"So... what's next?" said Mohit, looking at her with big, shiny eyes, his head on his arms on the table. Ray got really irritated when someone tried to be all babylike around her. Perhaps the reason being that she was not appreciated herself as a child. But that was not going to allow her to be a bitch. She had disciplined herself all too well.

"What are you talking about? Aren't you going to have your lunch?" she said after swallowing her banana shake.

"Oh really? You don't know?" said Mohit again in that teasing baby voice.

Control... breathe...

Her **head** counsellor was really putting in the work.

"No, I really don't." she sipped immediately to hide her irritation.

"I meant, on your road to becoming a pilot or should I say runway to becoming a pilot?"

Ray never liked to talk about her future plans with anyone. She would not even actively think about it until she needed to act on something. Everything worked in the background. Constantly.

"It'll be a one week affair, 5-6 days for the selection board interview and the remaining time for travel."

"Yeah... I know about that. One of my cousins had talked about it in lengths in front of the whole family of ours and we all thought that he was going to make it. He seemed so sure."

He waited for Ray to say something but Ray was least interested in knowing what happened with his cousin. But she let it slip, "So?"

"He didn't get through," he said morbidly.

"Next time." She did not let what she heard get from her ear to her head.

"So, have you talked to the HR about the leaves that you'll be taking?"

"Yes, I have and in fact they've allowed me an off for eight days," Ray said triumphantly.

"Awesome! You'll have a lot of time to go sightseeing after finishing up the rounds," he said enticingly.

"No... I don't think so. I'll come back right away," she said in a polite but defensive manner.

Mohit got the hint. "I really wish that you do great and don't forget me after you become a pilot."

"That's so silly, I never forget people." She wanted to say friends but did not want to rub him the wrong way.

"Then you'll definitely not forget me."

"Let's get back to our systems, time's up."

A few days later...

"Wish I had someone to accompany me."

She had to catch her train the next day. Ray was keeping track of all the articles and essentials she will be needing for the event. She was being frantic and doing things hurry scurry.

"Where's the toothpaste... Ouch! Oh God."

The toothpaste had slipped from her hands and fell onto her foot. She ignored the waning pain.

" ... And snacks?" Ray looked all around her room but she couldn't find anything but the heaps of misplaced and displaced things.

"Where's my charger?!"

Ray saw a cable hanging out from beneath the pile of clothes. She dragged it too furiously and it hit her in the face. She felt her lower lip go hot suddenly. She looked in the mirror and there it was, a pool of blood that had started to form in her mouth. Seeing it flipped something inside her and everything that had been boiling inside of her, spilled out of the brim. She fell down on the floor and that fall was the fall of her guard too. Ray wailed and cried.

"Why? Why?"

This time, her pain had broken out of the safety fence in her head and that pained her even more, having defied her own discipline.

"Why am I left alone? I can't take this anymore. I can't. I can't take this. What is the point of me having anything? What's the point of me going there? What's the point of it all when I don't have anyone to share it with. My parents? Neil? What's the point if I get through?"

But the thought of getting through suddenly made her stop.

Getting through.

Ray felt those words again and she stood up. She looked in the mirror again and dabbed the blood. Ray thought she looked really cool with blood red lips; like a vampire. She narrowed her eyes and took in the 'red eyes and blood-red lip look.' Ray realized her own stupidity and giggled. But the pain of feeling alone was not quite gone.

"I'm getting through this, and I'm getting through this pain too. There will be a day when I won't need the pills. When I won't need to worry about whether I'm going to feel okay or not, whether I'm going to cry or not or whether I'm going to be silent or not heard. There will be a day when I'll be truly happy and that too for no reason at all. Just happy."

A happy Ray.

And Ray wiped the remaining tears and blood away. She decided to take the complete dose of medication this time to make sure that she does not wake up mid-sleep. She packed her bags, took the dose and plugged in to her favorite songs.

"All the best," Mohit texted.

She closed her eyes, smiling.

Chapter 25

THE ORATOR

Ray reached the address on the call letter fifteen minutes early. She was thankful that the reporting time was in the afternoon and not in the morning and she had been able to get enough sleep.

There was a huge crowd of people. Some of her age but mostly looked older than her.

There were only two more girls that she could spot there. They both seemed to be discussing something from a little orange book.

Ray noticed a lot of guys noticing her. One group, she saw from the corner of her eye, had been laughing looking directly at her. She felt sorry for them for such people had no respect in her eyes. Ray thought of joining the girls but an announcement was made abruptly:

"All candidates, get your documents ready for verification. Please stand in a queue."

Everyone instantly followed the directions, Ray found her place in the line when a fellow candidate offered her a spot in front of him. She smiled at him and stood comfortably. Ray checked her documents one more time and when done, she looked behind her to find that the other two girls had been standing right behind her. She smiled at them too and waited for her turn.

When the verification was done, the candidates were taken to a bus that was going to take them to the selection board center. Ray was immediately offered a seat along with the other two girls by two fellow gentlemen. She let the two get seated first and then sat herself.

"I'm Rayveena, are you guys sisters?"

The two girls, each in glasses and braids with messy hair looked at her in disbelief.

"How did you know?" They asked.

"I mean you look similar... kind of." Ray did not want to make it awkward.

"Yes. We're sisters. I'm Niti and she's Suniti you don't have any book or notes..?"

"I have it in my bag, just needed to get a breather from all the travelling," she lied(...).

"Oh. Okay." And they went back to digging in the pages. Ray didn't even want to look at what they were reading and become antsy.

They reached the center and on the entrance, there were life-sized models of tanks and missiles that she was seeing for the first time. On looking at them, she felt something unfamiliar, something which was bigger than herself— a selflessness.

Inside, they were given a briefing and their documents were checked once again.

Their screening test was to be held the next day. All of them were given cutouts to wear which had a number on them each. Ray was candidate number 16. She had wanted something like a 7 but at least 1+6 is 7. She smiled to herself.

She saw that the seats were being filled up from the back so she got herself seated in the first row with no worries at all.

The intelligence rating test was to be held in a few minutes. They were given a booklet with multiple choice questions and twenty minutes of time. Ray went through the booklet once, it had fifty-five questions. She had no doubts she could do it and jumped right in.

The next round for the day was picture perception test to be followed by a group discussion.

They all were shown a black and white picture of a guy who was lying ill in a bed with a mask on and there was a doctor beside him who was on a call with someone. He had a mask on too.

They were all given five minutes to write a story based on the picture. As soon as the timer started, all the candidates started scribbling. There was this sudden silence in the room and Ray was grateful for it. She picked up her pen and peered at the image in an attempt to find something beyond the obvious. She allotted herself one minute to do that.

The mask—the recent pandemic—the doctor can't be so irresponsible to talk on the phone while attending to a patient that serious—his eyes are crinkled—the mask is stretched around the cheeks— there's a television and it shows a happy news anchor—the patients expression is relaxed—

Then, it clicked—

They found the cure!

Ray looked at the clock immediately, thirty seconds had past. She started writing everything in a coherent manner and finished it in four minutes. In the last minute remaining, she busied herself with visualising the group discussion they were about to have.

During the group discussion, the instructor told the candidates to narrate their stories one by one starting from the back. Ray heard the stories one by one and was amazed by the length of content that those people had been able to write. One guy was stuttering but his story seemed to relate to the picture more than the others'.

The two sisters in the back narrated stories that were very slightly different. Nonetheless, everyone seemed to be picking up on a pessimistic storyline and Ray picked up on that and then, came her turn.

She picked up her paper and put it down instantly knowing that she had not much to read from. Ray turned halfway towards the back and started speaking impromptu, "This story seems to be relating to a recent pandemic that hit our world unfortunately. And it seems as though a cure has been found in the scenario shown and let me line out why:

1. The news anchor seems to be delivering a good news.

2. The doctor's expression is also suggesting that he's got a good news from someone.

3. The patient's expression is also seemingly that of relief. So I gather that the doctor has already attended to the patient and will soon be cured by the newly found vaccine." ... And her time was up.

There was a deathly stillness in the room. The same stillness that she was welcomed with in school and university which immediately used to lead to a thunder of claps. But there was no time alloted here for applauds and the instructor immediately moved onto the next candidate.

When everyone was done, they were made to sit in a circle to start the group discussion. The aim of the discussion was to reach a common storyline. One tall, buff guy with a defined face, who was being stared at continuously by Niti, spoke up first. "I would like to open this discussion by putting forward my thoughts on this picture. I think that the patient is critically ill and it's showing the irresponsibility on the doctor's part. The patient seems dozed off and the news anchor could be talking just about anything. So I think this picture is a reflection of the system's irresponsibility," he said boldly.

The guy who was stuttering before jumped in the discussion, this time without stuttering.

"I would like to say that everything that we're seeing in the picture is... uh an important clue and the story seems to be more hopeful than my friend here is making it out to be. The news anchor is s-smiling that's an indicator of a good news and and if we relate it with the du-doctor, and the recent pa-pandemic, it definitely seems to be uh... an indicator of the invention of a vaccine," he said phlegmatically.

Ray released a sigh of relief upon hearing his optimistic views. Almost everyone was in consensus when Ray summed up the whole discussion.

"We all agree that the story suggests the invention of a vaccine for the virus that hit our world and I'd like to conclude with that. Thank you." Ray blinked her eyes after she said that; gratitude for the audience, she was taught, was the sign of a true performer. But she knew, this was no one man show, rather a team play.

A three-hour break had been announced and after that the selected candidates' names were going to be declared.

Chapter 26

NOT SO ALONE

Ray looked around and found Niti and Suniti who were chatting with the buff guy. She fluttered up to them like a fairy, glowing with a newfound happiness in her chest.

"Hey, do you guys want to go for lunch?" she asked.

"No actually, we have brought ourselves some." Suniti showed her a big lunch box indifferently.

Ray pretended to not feel an ouch.

"Oh okay, that's great." The light in her chest seemed to go dimmer.

"I haven't brought anything either so we could go together to grab something to eat," the buff guy said warmly and confidently. Ray couldn't refuse the offer of some company.

"Okay," was all she said.

"Okay then girls, I'll see you later. Bye." He waved at the sisters.

"Bye," added Ray with a hearty smile.

"So... You're Rayveena right?" he asked.

"Right."

"I'm Eesh."

"Eesh," Ray repeated.

Interesting name...

"Yeah but I write it as I-s-h. So, many people mistake it as Ish..."

Ray laughed. She gathered this was going to be a long conversation and there was nothing else she had to do to spend the rest of her time. So she played along.

"What would you like?" asked Ish.

"I guess, I'll have a milkshake."

"And?"

"And? That's it."

"What? You're not going to eat anything? It's been a long day," he said, concerned.

"No, I'm good." She put her hands in her pockets awkwardly.

"I'm ordering two meals. Okay?"

"Okay fine." Then she took out her wallet.

"Wait." And Ish pulled out some cash and handed it to the canteen keeper in no time.

"You're going to have to take the money from me," Ray threatened him by pointing her cash in his face as if it were a gun.

"Come, let's eat." He brushed it off playfully.

Ray started to nibble while Ish was eating like he had been hungry for ages.

He must eat a lot to maintain that body,

she understood and looked at her own slim but untoned body. A little belly was out but it was comfortably hidden under her T-shirt. Ray decided to not think about it. And she, too, started to eat in full portions. "It's good."

"Yeah."

That was the only conversation had during the meal and Ray liked it that way.

When finished eating, they decided to roam around the premises.

"Do you work?" asked Ray.

"Yeah actually, I work for Mindhouse the real estate company."

"Oh! that's a good company. I work for D-Ginnie."

"That's good too," said Ish with his eyebrows raised and face tilted.

Ish turned out to be friendlier than Ray had imagined. He kept talking and talking and she phased out. She now focused more on his demeanor and the psyche behind his every word. He was speaking in a slow and measured manner with a heavy depth in his voice, giving each word its deserved time.

So he weighs his words before talking... Sincere about his communication skills,

Ray deduced.

"I gave this idea to our managing director, and he immediately asked me to make a presentation, which he absolutely loved. And the next thing we know is that I was speaking to an audience of five-hundred people!"

"That's great." Ray decided not to talk about her own presentation that she had given in the intercollegiate competition, in front of a thousand people. She wanted to listen more.

He seemed to be someone who liked to impress women and made full throttle use of his looks too. Ray could not help but notice how he had managed to speak with the **girls** before any other guy. But he definitely seemed more ambitious than to spend all his energy on chasing pretty women.

"So?" Ish asked and Ray was pulled out of her meditation.

"Umm... no I don't drink. Never even tasted. Actually once I did, under peer pressure, but never felt interested myself."

"As you wish, totally. I never forced my girlfriend to drink. She forced me," he laughed.

He has a girlfriend...

Ray was a little annoyed and relieved at the same time.

"So, how's she..?"

Thank God, now I can make him talk about his girlfriend and the burden will be off of me.

The burden of him being even slightly interested in her.

"She *was* my girlfriend. Ex."

"Oh I'm sorry."

She did not know if she was sorry for him or herself.

"No. I'm not sad at all. Hey, give me your phone number," he said in a gentle yet authoritative manner.

Ray pulled out his phone from his breast pocket, "Unlock it."

Ish smiled at her and put his finger on the sensor while the phone was still in her hand. She dialed her number, hung up and put the phone right back in where it was.

They saw the crowd moving back to the hall and they moved along.

"It's about time," said Ish.

Her eyes caught some guys looking at her and then at Ish. It made her feel like puking for some reason.

How could they even think? We're just walking together. Typical...

They reached the hall and the names of selected candidates were being called out.

"Rayveena." Ray heard her name too soon. Ish patted on her back gently. She smiled back at him but it had not hit her yet.

"Ish," the instructor called out.

"Congratulations," Ray said luxuriously.

The selected ones were allotted new chest numbers and were required to fill up a questionnaire.

After the formalities, it was time to say goodbye for the day.

"Okay then, see you tomorrow," said Ray.

"Okay. Bye."

And they both started to walk away.

"Hey Ish!" Ray called out.

Ish looked back with a question on his face. "Check your pocket," she said, pointing to his breast pocket.

Ish looked inside and he was surprised to see the 250 rupees that he had paid for her lunch. He nodded his head in amazement.

"Will see you tomorrow," Ish threatened.

They both laughed.

Chapter 27

THE MOST CONTAGIOUS VIRUS—DOUBT

"So? How did it go?"

"Er, it wasn't bad I'd say. At least I got through the first stage."

"Really? I knew it."

"You're so sweet Sans. Hold up someone's calling... Leave it."

"Who's it?"

"Nothing it's just a guy I met to—"

"Oooooh finallyyy! Ray you met someone you like after so long! How does he look?"

"He looks fine and there's nothing like what you're thinking. He's probably trying to distract me you know. I can't trust someone I just met."

"You're right, focus on the game. Did you tell your mom about your day?"

"No, it didn't even occur to me. Anyways it's very late. They must be sleeping."

"You should sleep too, must be tired. Tell me everything tomorrow."

"I will Sans, bye."

"Byeh."

Ray headed inside to prepare her bed. The room she got seemed too big for her. For she was the only one in there and was thankful for it.

She had had enough experience to know that sharing space wasn't her thing. Back to her college days, she had been allotted a room with a girl who always seemed so chirpy, always on the phone and rather noisy. She would stay up talking and giggling till 3 a.m. while Ray tried to study and sleep by 11 p.m.

Ray confronted her one day, in a way as polite as possible with the frustration that had built up to the brim. And from the day onwards, the girl started to ignore her and brought two more of her friends into the room. And now, the three of them created three times as much the noise. Ray felt lonelier than before. The girls didn't change so she shifted to a separate room.

Fast forward to the place where she was currently living as a paying guest. Initially, she lived with two other, much older girls who always seemed to be delivering speeches about how horrific and absolutely victimizing their families were to them and how they couldn't bear to live in their homes anymore so they shifted to there. Ray never expressed her own plight to them.

She couldn't stand the fact that they used to be on their phones all the time, talking loudly to their parents, trying to act as their counsellors. But they could not keep their own for long and joined in the fight. Everything would turn very ugly, very soon. They would start shouting and cursing their own parents!

At times, the girls even switched families to offer their piece of mind.

In a way, Ray understood their situation and tried to sympathize and cheer them up. But they seemed to be more interested in taking her advantage. Always making her do one thing or the other for their own sake. They would go to the market for a nice time and by the time to return, Ray would realize that she had bought the least number of items and yet her bag was the heaviest, filled with their stuff.

The day she realized that the environment in that room, too, was toxic for her, she feared history repeating itself and shifted to a separate room.

The girls were shocked when they found out. They couldn't make out why the sweet girl had decided to move out. Ray had never said anything confrontational thinking it might make things even worse just like what happened the last time when she had shared space. So she just moved out quietly.

And now, she had **only** her own misery with her at least. No one to add to it. No one to take away from it. She was happy that her time was really hers and that was wealth to her.

Time is money.

***

Lying on her bed in the allotted room, she was going through it all and came back to her **now**.

She was there alone.

Again.

She smiled at how situations always seemed to repeat. Her phone rang and it was not Ish as she had expected. It was Mohit.

She was happy that she won't feel alone anymore.

"Hi," she beamed and sat up.

"Hi miss, you forgot me too soon."

"No... I didn't. Obviously. By the way, what was your name again?" She wiped a tear from her cheek.

"Ha-ha not funny. I'm mister..."

"Ya?"

"Mister... mister."

"What? That's it?"

"Yeah, I'm whatever you want to call me."

Ray was taken aback a little. She was afraid that she might be sending the wrong signals to Mohit.

"Oh come on, I didn't mean it that way," said Mohit sensing the reason of her silence.

Mohit's carelessness with his words always irritated her but she let him off for too long, for he wasn't **that important** to her. Ray felt that her spirits were down already, she didn't want to talk to him anymore and failed to understand why her emotions were on mission override.

"No... it's just that I'm a little tired so that's slowing down my responses, maybe." She still had to keep it decent because no matter what, he wasn't a bad person.

"Oh ya, I totally forgot to ask, how did it go?"

"I got through the first stage and I'm the only girl here now, in this center at least, in this room even. I also met this guy, works for a big real estate company and he's been calling me too many times, I'm totally bothered." She said that—

1. to draw attention from her most recent achievement and

2. to burn Mohit so that he never dares to be lovey-dovey with her.

"That's great, you've already made a friend there." He didn't say anything about her fresh success and it baffled her because it only made him predictable.

She hated it when guys steered wherever she nudged them to be.

"No, he's not a friend, I just met him. So how are things in the office? Anything new?"

"Well, I was going to tell you about that."

Ray got guiltily excited to hear about some drama. "I'm listening."

"Are you sure, that, you're doing the right thing?"

Something inside her snapped but she kept her composure. "What?"

"Just hear me out, okay?"

"What am I doing wrong?"

"It's not that you're doing something wrong, it's just that, are you sure you're going to get through?"

"What are you saying? Nobody can know that before time. So how can I? I don't know if you trust me in this or not but I do, I'll do whatever I can."

"I know you can definitely do it but... I'm only trying to help you out."

"And how, exactly?"

"Okay don't get angry but, I overheard something." He said grimly.

Ray felt grimmer so she started to really breathe. A part of her urged her to not hear whatever it was and hang up, but she kept on the call.

"The company is going through a critical time right now and targets have been doubled, almost and so is the work. So..."

"So? I'll get to it as soon as I get back." She couldn't understand what he was trying to convey.

"Yes, but I heard that whoever is absent during this stage, or fails to perform will be laid off."

"Do you mean to say that they'll cut me off? Impossible! I have the official approval for my leaves!"

"I know that but—"

"Wait a second, who did you overhear?"

"Viyona."

"What?" Ray zoomed out into a state where she was trying to make out if Viyona could really lay people off and the answer came out to be a no. Not because of anything that Viyona had done but more because of the fact that she believed in the good in people. "No, she won't do that."

"She said everyone means everyone."

"This can't be, I'll call her and ask myself. Thanks for telling me. I'll get back to you. Okay?"

"Okay," said Mohit half-heartedly.

"Bye." She waited for him to say something but he didn't and she hung up.

Ray kept trying Viyona's number but it was switched off. She called the HR manager too and his number was busy. Finally, she left a message on Viyona's number.

Ray felt like crashing her phone on the wall but instead, kept it beside her pillow. She lied down and kept looking at the phone, waiting for a message or a callback.

Tired of waiting for five minutes, Ray dialed Mohit's number. It, too, was busy and she abruptly stood up and started to pace in the room.

It can't be, I have the permission, they can't do that to one of their best employees.

But you aren't experienced enough and moreover, nobody knows what Viyona might do.

I'm the best in my team. It's illogical to fire me.

Remember that time when she suddenly let an employee go?

Yeah, but I heard he'd misbehaved with a client. That's why. I should try her number one more time.

Again, switched off.

What if I don't make it to the end here and get fired from my work too?

The possibility made her stupefied.

"No." Her breathing was now heavier than before and she put her hand on her chest intuitively.

"I'm going to make it. I'm going to make it. It's all going to be fine."

She looked at her phone again, nothing and the doubt found a home in her mind. It wasn't going to be fine. Ray shut her eyes. She put her head in her hands one moment, and clutched her shoulders another.

Her body was going restless and there were a thousand bees of chaos buzzing in her head. She couldn't think, she forgot how to move and a storm had emerged inside of her which she had no control over. Ray tried to breathe deeply but the sobs were breaking in. She was bawling in pain.

Ray thought of looking at the time but also knew that there won't be any time left now for her to sleep peacefully. She had to take the pill but it could give her a brain fog the next day and that might prevent her from thinking clearly during her psychology tests. But if Ray doesn't take the pill, she won't be able to sleep well and perform in the physical.

She felt even deeper in it, seeing the odds piling up against her.

Fifteen minutes had passed. Her head was now hurting and her body exhausted. She lied down with her eyes dead and staring at the dead white wall with nothing to focus on. It seemed to her, like the wall was as barren as her own heart was. Nothing, she had, to make it the centre of her life and it reminded her of Neil. But this time only the worst memory had decided to visit her.

Chapter 28

SELF-RESPECT?

"Where were you Neil? Are you okay? I've been calling you for twenty days!"

Ray was heart broken but still wanted to give him a chance to explain himself, to convince her in such a way that could make her twitching self-respect go away. She wanted to choose Neil over anything, she just needed a reason.

"You've been calling me incessantly. It's causing a lot of distraction. So I called to ask you, what do you want?" Neil said coldly.

It wasn't the Neil she knew, not until now.

"Why are you talking like this?" she said in a cracking voice. She couldn't stop her tears from welling up.

"I always talk like this."

"No, you don't talk like this," she said in an attempt to remind him of his own affection that was lost somewhere now.

"I didn't call to hear your sobs. Just tell me how will you stop calling?"

She was about to ask him to block her right away instead but she didn't want that. "So this is how you're now?"

"What are you saying? I was always like this," he said with such conviction that it made her doubt her own memory. She tried to overcome the disbelief and came up with some words—

"Why didn't you pick up?" she pleaded.

Ray couldn't help but remember all those nights when she had called him numerous times each day and each day, nobody picked up.

She had texted him hundreds of questions, requests, pleas and testaments of her love for him and of his love for her.

Ray couldn't fathom the fact that her world, had suddenly gone somewhere, away. Never for once, she doubted that she was his world too and he had done more than just proving it to her.

"I have work to do," he said with an air of supremacy.

"So? You don't even have five minutes now?"

"I do, that's why I called and so make it quick and answer my question."

"No you answer mine, what has happened to you? What do you think of me? You didn't think, even for once, about what I might be going through? Haan?" Her breath wasn't steady.

"You can stop your whining and answer my question otherwise I'll have to hang up," he dared her and she didn't want him to go.

"Fine. I'll answer your question if you answer mine."

"I'm not bound to."

"How's your work?"

"It's great as usual."

"How are your parents? They must be proud of you for such a catch of an employer."

"Yes, Vel-E is the biggest software company in the world. What else do you expect?"

"Right." She didn't have the competence to match his smugness. Ray had never seen him that way.

To her, he was someone she loved, not someone she would want to compete with. She only loved him.

Sensing the silence, she asked more.

"So... what are your future plans?"

"All lined up. I might move out of the country in less than a year."

"Wow, that's awesome. Really." She was truly happy upon hearing that and it hit her hard that in his perfect life, she wasn't invited.

"So... you'll be making a new girlfriend there," she teased. Ray had an amazing ability to gather up all her energy when it came to cheering up Neil but it didn't touch him.

"I don't have much time."

"Okay then, tell me you don't remember anything. Those moments we had together?"

"I have no time for this. Bye." And he hung up.

Ray couldn't believe it. She sat with her mouth open in disbelief and her cheeks were being run over by silent tears.

"He's done it again. He really has changed. No wonder, he was always the better one. He deserves a life, of his dreams."

She dialed his number again. Nothing. Twice, nothing. Fifth time, he picked up.

"Listen, I don't have time for your negativity."

Ray was taken aback by his strong voice. She had never heard it before.

"I just wanted to know what happened," Ray said in a determined voice. Her soul was now ready to know everything that Neil wasn't telling her.

"You really want to know?"

"Yes."

"Forget it."

"Just tell me, goddamn it!"

"See? This is the whole reason. Your impulses. Whenever I talk to you, you're just... so... **negative**, always deep in sorrow. Every other day you're crying or you're pretending like someone's out there ready to get you. I'm done listening to your whining. Nothing makes you happy. How much do I sacrifice my own time and life to accommodate to your melancholy?"

Her mind had gone silent and she liked it. She had gotten her answer. It was hard to believe that her biggest supporter had had enough of her but the chase for an answer had finally ended.

"You could've just let me know. I'd have left your life happily. Doesn't matter, I'll do it now."

"Doesn't matter to me. I have work to do."

"I'm really happy for you and I'm sure your future is going to be even brighter."

"No doubt."

Ray was not finding any end to his indifference so she decided to ask him the last thing she needed to know but didn't want to know.

She mustered up all her courage and breath and asked him, "So you don't want me anymore?"

"No."

The answer was too quick and emotionless. She was in disbelief. Only the last nail in the coffin was left now.

"You don't... love me?" she asked in a dying voice and for a moment, she wished that he stayed quiet. She never wanted to hear the answer. Her breath had stopped, her mind was full of nothing. She wished she was ready but she wasn't. Ray shut her eyes and clutched her arm.

"No."

She put the phone aside and sat there on the bed with her legs curled up. There was a smile on her face. Then a moment later, her eyebrows got tensed. She smiled again but with tears this time. A hot stream of tears came out and then stopped at once. She breathed in clearly and accepted it. Accepted the fact that the very person who made her feel alive didn't want to accommodate with her deepest feelings.

Why?

The question couldn't help but pop up.

Because he deserves a better life, a better girl.

What about me?

Just have to... live with this poison balked halfway in my throat, for the rest of my life.

I saw the rest of my life with him.

And she didn't know how to counter that.

Chapter 29

DEPRESSION

After that day, Ray didn't know who to talk to or who to confide in. Her overwhelming emotions never left her side. She didn't know what to do with them. Ray would break into tears randomly and her parents were growing impatient with her.

Her condition became worse; lying all day in bed, not being able to move her body like she used to. She put her feet on the ground but didn't feel them. Her incessant sorrow and the medication had made her numb. She didn't desire anything, she didn't want anything. Nothing made her angry. Nothing soothed her aching soul and the doctor kept on increasing her dose.

Her hands trembled, her face was always puffy. She would try to put on a face for the guests but then she would get exhausted right after that.

Her soul had forgotten itself. If someone were to ask what food she liked, she would go clueless and say just anything that came into her mind. The world had lost its colours and sweet illusions. There was nothing she wanted. All she did was cry and sleep and eat, then lay in the bed and cry and sleep. On weekends, her psychiatrist would visit her. He was trying his best.

One day, he asked her to open up. "Is there anything else that's bothering you? Any incident that affected you specifically? Something you just can't seem to unremember?"

And Ray felt a balloon inflating in her chest. She knew something was wrong but she was not the one to blame anyone for her suffering. Always forgave people, always giving them second chances but that day, something inside her mind didn't want to be hiding anymore. She thought she might die with this pain inside of her and no one will ever know. There was nothing to look forward to. She had no hopes of ever smiling a real smile. How was it possible? For someone to be so empty inside.

No. She wasn't empty. There was that grim darkness that kept poking inside.

"Sometimes, I feel like... like I... I don't think that I should've been born." The words came out very stickily from her soul.

"Why? You're a well educated and a capable young woman." The doctor honestly wanted to know.

"Because... I... I know that I can do some good things and I have done them in the past. I was a good student and I tried to be a good daughter too."

Her arms felt as if invisible snakes were crawling in them and she pressed them while she struggled to talk.

"How's your relationship with your parents. How are they towards you?"

She was taken aback by the question. "They're good people but I don't think they like me."

"Why do you think so?"

"Because I'm like this. But I promise... I try to fight it, I try to really understand why this happens but I don't know when it overtakes everything, my emotions and my body."

"They're your parents and you're their responsibility. It's their responsibility to take care of you when you're sick and right now, you're just sick. There's nothing wrong with you or your personality. I need you to understand that."

Ray kept nodding nervously all the while the doctor talked.

"I know, but whenever it feels like I'm recovering, something happens."

"Like what?"

"I..."

"Don't worry, it's just between me and you."

"I try to help my mother with everything but it doesn't seem to be good enough for her or my father. I know that they want me to work to compensate for all the money they spent on my education, and I... I try to... but it's too heavy. I can't concentrate on anything."

The doctor noticed uncannily that she was slouching and constantly holding her arms as if she was protecting her body from something.

"Has anyone ever raised a hand on you?" he said sympathetically.

Ray went silent... her eyes shot to that place on her arm where she had made slits with a blade because her parents had given her an ultimatum to not talk with anyone on the phone. She had grown fitful because all she had was that one friend who she could tell her feelings to and confide in. She remembered several other times when her parents told her that they wished she were dead. It wasn't like she was being physically abused by them but yes, she felt mentally and emotionally hurt **everyday.**

"No… but their words hurt," she said without any emotion.

"What do they say and what for?" he pressed.

"Simple. They wanted a son." She smiled.

"That's a very, very biased way of thinking about their own offspring. What can't girls do today? They're doing everything that boys do."

"That's right, but at least, they allowed me an education. Even though they never really appreciated any of my medals or trophies. They were so done with me that they even—" She had gone too deep into her unadressed emotions.

"Hmm?"

"I can't, it's too painful."

"Just let it out," he sympathized.

Ray looked around to see if her parents were there.

"Well, they sometimes say that they would've been happier if I wasn't born in the first place. And that they'd rather have a boy."

Ray cleared her throat and her breath was better. She was speaking her truth.

"And my grandma told me that they had even decided to abort me. But she was against it. So fatefully, because of her, Rayveena came into this world uninvited. A world where she didn't want to be in the first place. Because of my grandma." She smiled genuinely remembering her. "She used to say that I was Lakshmi born into her house. For some odd reason she thought that I was very lucky. It has been very hard since she died. I feel unwanted, a burden. Like I'm not supposed to be here. I don't feel like smiling or laughing like other people of my age. Nothing feels worth it. Doctor, I beg you please don't tell all this to anyone. I have forgiven them but the memories still hurt sometimes."

The psychiatrist was deep in contemplation before he said, "You have a really big heart for forgiving them. My only suggestion for you is that you should get better as soon as possible and move forward in life. Become independent and stay with your friends. Any boyfriend?"

"I had one and I used to tell him everything and he too, supported me. But we broke up and it's harder now without his support. I'm not sad because he left me. I wasn't supposed to be a problem for anyone. It's his life. I'm just sad that I have no one to talk to."

Ray wondered if she had said too much.

"Hmm. You're a very strong person. And a good person. It takes a lot to forgive our own people. But what you need to learn is how to forgive yourself." He glanced at her arm slightly. "You have a really big heart. I wish you all the luck in your life. And continue with these medications. Tell me how you feel the next time we meet. Okay?"

"Okay," Ray smiled back.

Chapter 30

ICARUS FALLS ON SOFT CONCRETE

Ray had spent so much time reminiscing and being lost in her past that the feelings had become overwhelming now. She broke into tears but this time she was going to be taking no chances.

"Flub it! Come what may."

And she popped the pill she hated, that she had kept securely in her bag. She didn't want to exhaust herself anymore.

A few minutes later, the street light outside the window started to move and blur. And it all went black.

***

The next day, she had no other intention in her mind than to get through the day, victorious. Again.

Ish was also there but he didn't look at her. She didn't care. If she feels like talking to him later on, she will let him know. But for now, she was single mindedly focused.

The candidates were shown a dozen pictures. Each, they had to observe for twenty seconds and then write a story based on that within four minutes. She did that in a spell, no problem. Time was running fast for her today. Ray did not know when she got started and when she reached the last picture.

The word association test was next and that too, was done in a moment. Then, came the situation response test in which they had one minute to write their response to a given situation. Done in a second!

Ray felt an aggression that had been built up in her and she was channeling it well in the tests. Then came the hardest part, self description test which was all about how her parents and friends saw her. And how she herself saw her. Ray felt like she had to lie here. This test was also completed but somewhere in her mind, she was worried that she might get caught in her lies.

Come on! Stop thinking like a whiny kid.

She was growing impatient with herself. Her own worry and aggression was piling up against her. She wasn't thinking clearly. She feared she might have a brain fog at the physical test. She was nervously pressing her fingers trying to control the snakes that seemed to crawl under her skin.

It's here!

The dark cloud. Her eyes went lifeless in a split second. She felt her anxiety growing on her and she had no time to deal with it.

The candidates were called to the field and were shown a series of obstacles that they would have to cross within two attempts.

She didn't look at them all; only the first one which was a very thin staircase of five steps. She felt a wobbling in her feet by just looking at them. Then she tried to remember her morning jogs and jogged a little on the spot to warm up. In her mind, she looked like a little chick pedaling on the ground among some huge smug hens. She grew conscious of her body even when no one was looking at her.

Maybe they'll give me another chance?

She felt a little guilty for playing the woman card in her head.

One by one, the guys came and showcased their fitness and reflexes on the obstacles. She felt a little relaxed but guiltily, when she saw a couple of guys falter on the staircase. They were not going to make it. She used to think that all guys were tough.

Ray looked at her shoes to make out exactly how she was going to place them on the steps.

Her turn came and she put her first foot on the step exactly as she had imagined and pushed up to the next one but before she could take the another step, her body went out of balance and she hardly managed to not fall.

Plan change!

Ray was now going to let her feet decide how to move. Her whole body was burning and as she had feared, the brain fog arrived and she had lost all desire to move. Suddenly, Ray didn't want to do this anymore. She wanted to turn back and go back to her room and lie on the bed. Her body went limp and the weight of ambition was nowhere to be found. Her body was now shutting itself down.

No. I have to do this. For myself!

Only the voice in her head was as strong as before. She put one foot after the other and went up. As she rose, so did her hopes with her. And an image of her grand success was formed in her mind immediately, she got overwhelmed by it and faltered on the last step. This time, she let herself fall back on the ground without fighting for balance. **The ground wasn't so harsh.**

The instructor came to Rayveena's aid and asked her if she had been injured. She shook her head and stood back up with his help.

"Don't worry, you have other obstacles to score more."

But she didn't want to go on. Her body had no motivation, no kick, no adrenaline. Ray wished she hadn't taken that goddamned pill. The next obstacles had no mercy on her either. Her feet were shaky, her body felt too stretched and too exhausted and slow. She just wanted to fall back on something.

Shortly afterward, the group tasks started but the candidates' enthusiastic calls sounded like shrill noises to her. She didn't participate in any decision making and let the others decide. Ray hated it. She hated that she had given up. But she could not hate herself.

***

Ray came back to her room relieved now that she could let all her weight fall back on the bed. She knew she wasn't going to be called for the personal interview. But she wasn't worried anymore. Ray didn't care about anything but the fact that she was safe in her bed without any judgements or scores being credited to her fragile body and mind. Ray was proud of herself for getting this far. She will get another chance the next year.

After hours, her body was back to normal and she felt her energy back and building up, she came to her senses. Now, she again wanted to ace the personal interview and impress the panel. But the chances were thin.

But I was the only girl there and I'm sure they will be impressed by my performance in psychology tests.

Her mind was racing, trying to convince her of a brighter picture but there was nothing that she could do now. Ray knew not to indulge in wishful thinking. She packed her things and didn't decide to roam around the city having seen enough. All she wanted, all she wanted was to be back in the **safety of less challenges.**

"Congratulations," she texted Ish.

She was sure he was going to make it.

Chapter 31

GRAVITATIONAL PULL

She came back to her room and decided not to give a thought to the past few days. She had never failed at anything in her life. Ever. And it was something that she wanted to keep at a distance from her consciousness.

Ray knew that she had another chance but she wasn't sure if she really wanted to take it. Everything had been put on the back burner for God-knows-how-long. Ray was just relieved now that she was back.

She didn't care much about what she was going to say to anyone because no one could understand what had happened to her. So Ray was going to tell the truth anyway. She did not make it and she was not upset.

Ray slept uneasily. Her body was fine, her mind wasn't feeling any trouble. Still, something inside was not letting her rest.

But she had already chosen her ego's comfort over the soul.

She woke up late and got dressed in whatever clothes she could find first in her cupboard and didn't take a bath. She put her hair up in a messy bun. Her car wasn't starting so she took the metro. She traveled half the ride standing and all crunched up.

At the next station, most of the ladies departed and before anyone could enter, the emptied seats were won in races. Ray kept standing where she was;

didn't care to sit. It did not make much of a difference to her. When did she ever feel comfortable in her life? Neil's thought came to her and she brushed it away frustratingly.

She punched in and felt hopeful about seeing the familiar faces. She sat in her usual seat and waited for Mohit's arrival. He was running late.

Nonetheless, someone else came by and Ray smiled at her— Daisy, held her hand but didn't shake it. Instead, they kept holding each other's hands lazily while they talked. Ray was looking up sitting in her seat. Anyone who walked by would have thought they were the best of colleagues.

"You're back haan…"

"Yes I am." Ray was forcing herself to seem happy.

Daisy wasn't reciprocating. She dropped the question, "But where were you all this time? How did you get leaves for so many holidays?" Daisy played aloof while enquiring.

"I had my Selection Board Interview."

"Oh, what's that?"

"That's the next round you need to clear in order to become an Air Force pilot after you've cleared the written test," Ray explained naturally.

"Oh and you didn't make it there?"

"Yeah I didn't. But there's another chance next year."

"Oh good, by the way, I got the highest incentive for this month. How much did you make?"

"That's great. Congratulations. Actually I don't know I'll have to check."

"Yeah, thanks."

Mohit arrived and he immediately smiled at Ray. She was relieved to see him.

"Hi Mohit," Daisy squeaked and extended her hand towards him. Mohit shook hands with her and immediately turned to Ray.

"Well miss, you seem a little tan." And he shook her hand. Ray felt self-conscious by the remark but let it go with a smile.

Daisy interrupted, "How much is your incentive this month, Mohit? You were on top last month." She looked at him in a sly and flattering way.

"Oh man, I couldn't really focus this time you know. Don't know why?" He started combing his hair with his fingers. Ray smiled. She wished she could be as relaxed as him sometimes.

"I understand totally. I too felt the same the last month but you know time, time is the key," Daisy added.

"Yeah, congratulations for this month again," he said.

Then he turned to Ray. "So, tell me more about your adventures miss pilot."

"Oh I forgot to turn my system on." Daisy paced away.

"What?" Ray asked Mohit who was still looking at her. "There was no adventure. I lost."

"Shut up! You can't lose, you're the best."

"Ha-ha right, but still, I lost. I was the only girl there."

"The guys must've swarmed you."

"No. It wasn't like that. Hey you told me about Viyona—"

"Ssh! Lower your voice."

"Okay. I called her several times but she didn't pick up. Do you think she's going to show up today? I need to clarify everything."

"No, I don't think she's coming but you should not be bothering about that now. You know our coordinator, he'll take care of it for sure."

"Okay..." Ray relaxed for the moment.

Ray tried to concentrate on her work but she was having a hard time. The images from the field, Ish, the sisters and the hall kept appearing. She decided she was going to ask the HR manager to clear her confusion, face to face after lunch.

***

"Hi Rayveena, how was your trip?" asked the HR manager cheerfully.

What trip?!

Ray entered his office and he motioned her to sit down.

"It was good but couldn't make it through the physical."

"Better luck next time," he said with a warmth that clearly showed on his chubby face.

"I actually wanted to ask you about something."

"Yes?"

"Is there any chance of layoffs happening?" She tried to read his face.

"Layoffs? And without me knowing?" He clearly looked surprised.

"I mean do you think something like that could happen?"

"Not that I know of. But who said that to you?"

"Uh… Alright then. I guess it was a practical joke someone played on me, thank you. See you later."

"Okay, bye."

Ray came out relieved. She felt that either the HR manager was lying or *Mohit* was. She decided to confront him after office hours.

Here and there, Mohit kept nagging her while working. But Ray didn't pay much attention to him.

"Hey look! This meme is so funny," he chirped.

Ray looked at the phone in his hand. "Hmm."

"What's wrong with your face? Looks like a balloon! I need a pin. Wait."

He started looking for something pretentiously behind his desktop and under the table. Ray couldn't stop smiling. He suddenly looked up and Ray, with a poker face, was fixated on the screen again. He gave up and returned to his work.

As much as Ray wanted to confront him, she didn't even want to look at him after work. Ray knew if she started talking, she might make a scene and the last thing she wanted was to stress herself out. So she decided not to talk to him.

After work, when he had gone to freshen up, Ray found her opportunity and left quietly.

Chapter 32

CONFRONTATIONAL PULL

Mohit was calling her repeatedly. She felt a familiar tinge sprouting from her memory. The tinge that one suffers from when someone you care about does not talk to you even after countless efforts.

She picked up the phone and quickly said, "Hello." nonchalantly.

"Hey, are you alright? What happened to you? You went away just like that."

"Yeah, I had to buy some groceries," she lied.

"But you didn't even say goodbye."

"Okay, I'll say bye after this call."

"Why are you so angry? Are you upset with me? If there's anything, then let me know at least."

"Well if you insist, I asked the HR manager about what you told me."

"What did I tell you?"

"Really?" She couldn't believe he didn't know what she was talking about.

"About those layoffs," she blurted out with difficulty.

"God, I told you to not talk about it with anyone and still?"

"You didn't want me to ask Viyona so I asked him instead. What's the big deal? I didn't take anyone's name. Anyway, he told me that there was no such thing going to happen."

She waited for a reply.

"Then that's even better news for you and everyone else. Now let it go."

"I still don't understand why you said that to me when there wasn't a proof. You're not the kind to not know things. You've been working here for a while and you're very well familiar with the higher-ups too." Her words were clear.

"I told you, I just overheard her saying that, maybe something changed her mind."

"I don't understand. Do you have any idea of how much it affected me and my performance? I was so stressed. Why did you tell me that? Why did you tell me so when you didn't think it was actually going to happen?"

"I didn't want to do that to you. I know how much it could affect you."

"But you did. Does Viyona know about this? That you've been spreading lies about her? How about I should check with her too."

"No, you're not doing that," he asserted.

"And why not? I'm in such a dilemma right now. I can't lose this job. I have to be sure. And she isn't even picking up my call."

"You don't have to bother her. If the HR manager says he doesn't know about this then that means it's not—going—to—happen. Why can't you just let it go?"

"I'm going to ask Viyona about this and don't worry, I won't be taking your name."

"No, you can't."

"What is your problem? I will talk to her and you won't even be brought up in the conversation!"

"No, you can't do that."

"Why?!" she almost shouted.

"Because it was a lie," he gave himself up.

"So you accept it. I know it was a lie but why did you do that?" Ray was calmer.

"So that you don't go anywhere."

"What? Are you trying to say that you just wanted to keep me with you? How could you be so selfish Mohit? And I have no such feelings for you."

"I know that."

"You shouldn't have done this," her voice cracked.

And there was no sound to be heard.

"Don't cry, I know it was important for you, but look at the bright side, you're going to have a great future here, you're one of the best we have."

"You don't understand. You can't! I wish I could forgive you more easily. I don't want to work here anymore. I'll find somewhere else to be."

"Listen, no you can—"

She hung up without listening to a word of his.

Chapter 33

TROUBLE, TROUBLE, TROUBLE

She had just stepped into her room when the phone rang.

"Hello?" she said, surprised. It was her mom. But she could feel something was off.

"Hello, Ray? I need you to come back home. Your father..." She suddenly started crying.

Ray was bewildered, it was all too fast for her to grasp.

"Mom stop crying, what happened to dad?" Her mind was blank and she tried her best to not let herself fret.

"You just come back here. God have mercy on me. Spare us. Why did you do this to me God?"

"Mom what happened? Where is he?"

"I'm in the hospital with him. You just come back here as soon as possible. God knows what happened to him. They say he had a heart attack. I don't know how this happened, he was all well in the morning went for work as usual then this?" she said, sniffing repeatedly.

Ray gave herself no time to be shocked or heartbroken. She had stilled her mind absolutely. "I'm coming."

It was late in the night but she didn't care. She locked her room and opened her phone to book a cab. Ray was breathing very deeply in order to keep herself steady. Her mind couldn't play any tricks on her now; no hoping for the worst, no crying. She was alert. The cab arrived in five minutes and she did not know when she got seated inside.

The cab had travelled more than halfway and she hadn't moved an inch in her seat. She just kept looking at the dark road in front of her.

Ray reached the hospital and looked around. Not a single soul was out there but the dogs that went about their nightly rambles. She didn't know if she was walking slow or fast. She didn't even know if she was walking.

Ray checked on the counter, and half-wished that his father's name weren't there. But it was.

"This isn't real," she told herself. She walked alongside the wall and turned inside. Ray had nothing to expect or to hope for but the sight of her father made things **real.**

She stood at the door and analyzed his body from afar. He was breathing and that made her breathe, finally. She hadn't taken a conscious breath in hours.

Ray walked into the room slowly and found her mother sitting in the corner, with her eyes closed. Nobody heard her footsteps. Ray walked up to her mother and lightly touched her on the shoulder. She didn't open her eyes and then Ray poked her shoulder slightly. Her mother opened eyes as if she were still in a dream.

Sometimes, to Ray, her mother looked like a dream herself. As if there was something unreal about her. Ray never understood why. But she was not unreal in a bad way. She felt unreal to her because Ray couldn't really figure her out. She would just keep on looking and gazing in order to grasp something or anything about the soul that her mother was.

Her mother looked at her with half-swollen eyes and grief-stricken face. For a moment, Ray didn't know why she felt that they might just smile at each other but nobody did.

Ray's mother had a kind of face that looking at, nobody could actually tell how old she was. She looked too young to be forty-five. She didn't have any cheeks but she had cheek bones. Her skin's epidermis had become like a plastic bag, shiny and with little flesh underneath. Her lips had a natural smile to them but they didn't seem happy now. She was plump but looked weak. Sometimes, Ray saw her own face in hers.

In her mother's childhood photos, Ray had discovered that her mother looked just like her, only a little taller and fairer.

"Did you eat anything?" Ray asked her.

"No." She didn't say it almost.

"I'll bring you something in a minute."

She put her bag aside and walked up to her father. He was sleeping. Ray couldn't imagine the pain that he must have gone through but strangely, there was a smile spread on his lips. He looked taller too. Or maybe she was imagining things. She took in a deep breath and decided not to ask about any details from her mother for both their sake.

"What will you eat, mom?" she asked meekly.

"Nothing, you can eat whatever you want."

"Okay." But Ray didn't go anywhere and sat beside her.

Ray looked at his father's weathered face. He was always smiling, she remembered from her childhood days. He had a strong nose just like hers. She looked at his hair and it reminded her of the unique dad-smell his comb had. He was dark with beautiful, perfect eyebrows just like hers. Ray couldn't help but smile. She smiled because he was fine now and smiling too, in his sleep. It did not matter that he had been in pain. She was just grateful that he was alive. Ray wanted to stay here with him and take care of him. She knew he wouldn't want that but the feeling in her heart was too strong. Ray looked at her mother who stared at something right above his father's nose. Maybe she, too, was reminiscing on the good olden days with her partner-for-life who was almost taken away from her.

Ray could not think of a moment in her life when her eyes were not able to find the sight of her father. Or her mother's. But that moment was going to show up sooner or later. That realization hit her right in the feels and sent chills down her spine. Just like a steel sheet reverberates when it is hit with a hammer. She decided she wasn't going anywhere else and was going to stay here with the first and true loves of her life.

Chapter 34

THE FAULT, DEAR BRUTUS, IS NOT IN OUR STARS BUT IN OURSELVES

"How's work going?" her mother asked. She was back to normal and was talking again.

"I am going to resign soon." Ray hated to remember what had happened with Mohit.

"That's good. Just stay here at home and we'll send you to your real home very soon. We have some good boys who've caught our eyes."

Ray wanted to say something back but decided to swallow it. She had hoped that her mother would ask her about the reason why she wanted to resign and then she would tell her all about how far she had actually been able to go in her pursuit.

Silly, why do you expect such things,

she chided herself. Ray looked for a moment at her mother and she couldn't help but ask, "What happened?"

"I don't know, I heard a thud and I came running out of the kitchen to find him lying on the floor, holding his chest. I couldn't understand! Just a minute ago he was having some water and was walking fine. And suddenly, he was like that? Only God knows what karma he's making me pay for."

Ray thought that her mother might cry at any moment now but she didn't and kept sitting there like a wounded soldier.

Ray blinked once and said, "At least, he's fine now."

***

The three of them were having dinner together after ages. Ray's father looked healthier. He was eating very slowly and silently, never looking up from his food. Her mother was, however, eating and talking rather normally.

"I had taken your birth details to the temple Pundit Ji—"

Ray stopped eating at once.

"He checked your kundli and said that there's a good yoga to get married next year and—"

Ray put her spoon down.

"He also said that you have a kalsarpa dosha in your kundli, but nothing to worry about, he told me the remedy for it too. You just have to—"

Ray stood up and went into her room without saying anything.

"See? This is the attitude of this girl. She won't let us live in peace. She resigned from her job and what does she want to do now? Does she want us to serve her all her life? For how long? So shameful it is. What will the people say? Relatives? She just keeps making us look down in front of the whole society." Ray's mother stopped to take a breath.

She took the dishes and threw them into the sink and didn't stop with her prickly and stinging remarks about her fateful daughter. Ray's father didn't say anything and went back to his bedroom but Ray had somehow hoped that he might say something.

She knew she couldn't stay. There was no peace here either.

She didn't have to go to the pundit. It's a shame that my own mother went to a stranger to know about her own daughter! What does he know about me? He knows his pseudoscience but he doesn't know me. What dosha? Am I just made up of flaws? Am I a sinner? No. I'm not. Nobody knows me more than me. He can keep his knowledge, I'll keep my life.

Later in the night, Ray went to her father's room, he was lying there quietly. She thought of saying something to him but couldn't utter a sound to wake him up and just came back out of the room.

"I guess, I'll just leave again without telling them."

Chapter 35

POWER PLAY

Ray didn't feel like getting up from her bed but she had to. She felt that she might fall back when she finally stood up. Ray had to work until she finds something else to do. Resigning wasn't her top priority for today.

If she made it to the office, that will be more than enough. She wished she could go on a long vacation with someone. Someone she cared about. But the thing is, she was scared to care now. She had been burned several times and did not want to get it all repeated with another person.

She reached office, Mohit was sitting there in his usual place. Ray looked at him but he seemed completely drowned in work. Out of nowhere, Viyona's secretary called her up.

"Viyona is asking for you," he said.

She was ready to go inside but couldn't decide whether she wanted to ask Viyona why she had not responded to her multiple calls. Or was Viyona going to ask her about that? Or could it be worse? Was she going to tell her to resign? Ray had prepared herself mentally for that too. She tried to look at the brighter side.

Okay, at least I will get a break before my next job.

"Hi Viyona," she said cheerfully.

"Hi Rayveena, how was your trip?" she said, too cheerfully.

Trip?! There was no trip!

"It was good but I didn't make it to the end." Ray was now growing tired of saying that.

"Well, that's how it is you know, one door closes and another opens. That's how life is. Have a seat!" She gave Ray that reassuring smile of hers.

Suddenly, Ray knew that Viyona wasn't going to ask her to resign.

Mohit had really been lying.

She nodded in agreement.

"Rayveena, something came to my notice and I just wanted to talk to you about that. I don't like to stutter so I'll ask you right away. Are you resigning?"

Ray saw a threat in her eyes somewhere. She couldn't say anything.

"Are you having any problems here?"

Yes. She was. But with Mohit, not her!

"No... nothing."

"If there are any issues, you can discuss with me or the HR manager. We are the best in the world and we have the best people here if you need any kind of support. But resigning? I don't think it's a solution. Just tell me why... because I can't fathom why you're ready to leave the best. We have the best structure and the best working environment too. Just give me a good reason why you thought of this."

Viyona's words were unending and Ray wasn't ready to answer when she suddenly stopped talking.

Ray was at loss for words. "I... haven't... thought of such a thing." The words were very, very sticky in her throat.

"Listen, you're a good employee and I just want the best for everyone in my team. And so naturally, I want the best for you! A person of your calibre should never leave something in between. You must have at least three years of experience before you become good at anything. I know it, trust me. I was once there where you're now. You hear me?" Viyona said in a caressing voice but her eyes looked a little bewildered.

Three years? I didn't think of staying for such a long time.

"I understand. Thank you for your time." Ray just wanted to end the conversation ASAP.

"Oh dear, I'm always here for my team. Just remember what I said always."

"Yes. For sure."

Too eager!

And they both shook hands.

So Mohit told her. Great.

She called him after having her dinner.

"I can't believe you just did that," Ray burst out.

"Did what, exactly?" There was a smugness in Mohit's voice.

"You told her. What is it with you? Are you in your senses even? I couldn't believe you turned out to be such a stalker."

"Listen, if you have to leave, you can leave today and I wouldn't care. I am not one of those guys to stalk women," Mohit snapped.

"Fine, I'm going to resign," Ray lied just to see his response and continued, "... But before I do that, you need to give me a good reason why you sabotaged my focus. I was so close. Did I do anything wrong to you? Was it because I never accepted you as something more than a friend?"

"Enough! Viyona was the one who made me. Here, you got your answer? Now just let me live."

"What? Viyona? Why would she?" Ray suspected Mohit was still lying.

"She knew you're very gullible and sensitive and you'd get phased by that lie. She didn't want to lose any of her **human resource** because the company invests a lot of time and energy in its employees. And if you leave, it will definitely be a loss for the company given your portfolio. So she played that card deliberately," he said robotically.

"I don't believe this. And you agreed to do all of this? You became her pet?"

"I have to go."

***

Ray could only imagine Viyona's face when she sent her resignation in. She knew she was going to be summoned by her the next day.

Ray went in to find Viyona busy with some foreign delegates.

"We will be taking your leave now, miss Viyona," said one of the blonde men eagerly.

Ray waited outside for them to leave. As soon as they did, Ray beamed, "Hey Viyona!"

"Rayveena. I thought we had talked about this?" she demanded.

Ray kept quiet and Viyona started to rant again.

"Do you have the slightest idea of what you're doing? **You** or anyone can never find a better employer than me and still you choose to leave? Don't you know who Viyona is? And what she can do? Did you really think that you were going to find work somewhere else just like that? You don't know about my networks, my influence. You won't find work anywhere, dear Rayveena." She looked as if she was trying to fit all her body inside Ray's skull.

Ray still kept quiet.

Wow, she is being really mean for no reason. Wonder what the others will say if they saw her like this.

"The choice is yours. Either you work here, under me or you never find work anywhere. Don't say I didn't warn you." She leaned back in her chair and started playing with her diamond ring, smirking triumphantly.

Ray was disgusted with Viyona's utter exhibition of her true colours. She raised an eyebrow, as she always did whenever she saw an ego challenging her. But she had already decided to leave and there was no changing that decision so she was calm and collected. She knew exactly how to counter Viyona in her own way.

"Do your foreign clients know that you have been misleading them more than ever before by sending nonreal users or should i say, bot traffic to their websites and apps. And also, do they know that you have been charging them fraudulently for a service that doesn't even exist! It's an open secret in the company. It's just a matter of time before it comes out into the public eye." Ray looked her straight in the eye.

Viyona gave her a death stare. She was set on fire and her eyes clearly showed it. "Are you trying to threaten me? You will be sorry for this," she said it too loud, the employees outside might have heard her.

"Don't you dare raise your voice with me. If you make a scene, you will be the one facing repercussions, mam. I have proofs with me. And if you try to harm me in any way, I will make sure that I bring you onto the streets." Ray felt blood rushing in all her body but her head was still focused. She continued,

"And there is absolutely no leverage that you have over me now. Can't say the same about some of the snakes in your company."

Hey! I think we're done now. It's enough.

"What do you want?" Viyona said through her teeth.

"Nothing. Because a person like you has nothing for me. I know how you applied your alleged *years of experience* to keep your *human* resources in this *rat* wheel. I just want you to never repeat that with anyone else. Ever. Know, that just like you, others have ambitions too. I'll take your leave now."

Ray stood up from the chair wondering where she got all this power from.

She left on that day to never return ever.

Chapter 36

SWEET SORROW

"Ray, I'm coming to meet you."

"No… you don't have to take that much trouble."

"No. What are you doing in that room? You can't stay there forever. You have to go somewhere, do something, meet people and **live.** I'm coming to see you."

"No Sans—"

But Sanya had hung up.

It has been forty-five days since Ray last got out of her room. She would only go out for groceries or to take a stroll on the terrace in the evening. She would wake up for breakfast then again would go back to sleep only to wake up for lunch, watch some videos about random things that caught her eye, have evening snacks and then sleep again.

Some days, she didn't sleep till 6 a.m. in the morning. And no, it wasn't like her college days when she would stay up all night either studying or watching a movie. She didn't know why she was doing whatever she was doing. Ray didn't even want to know. She had no desires left in her.

Why am I still alive? There's no point.

There were deep slits on her wrist and thighs.

She was comforted by the fact that there was no one trying to mess with her now. No nagging parents cursing their fate and hers, no Neil who made promises to never leave her and then did. No Mohit or Viyona who played with her vulnerability and no one, not anyone full of insecurities, trying to bring her down.

She was **safe** from all of that. Ray was safe from her trust being broken again. And she relished in that fact.

Sanya would call her every week and whenever she asked her about her future plans, Ray would go, "I don't know."

She really didn't care. All she cared about was her heart's safety above all. Her parents never bothered to call her.

One time, her mother called to enquire about what she was doing next and she was like, "I don't know." Her mother butchered her with words on hearing that. "Why don't you just die. You're no special to stay without marrying all your life. What do you even do in that room? How much more comfort do you want? And who's paying for your expenses? Who is it that's spending on you? So that's why you're not marrying."

Ray would go speechless at the fact that how much she was misunderstood by her own family. So she never called them either.

Even trying to make them understand, was extremely exhausting and seemed somewhat wrong to her. She sold her car and had gotten enough to survive for five months without any work. So money wasn't a problem, for now.

But time was. The only thing that still worried her was how much time of her life she was letting go by, just like that. But what she wanted more for herself was healing. She just needed to take a breather and really figure out what was going on with her and she didn't care about what anyone else had to say, she was going to choose herself.

Ray hugged Sanya dearly as soon as she saw her. She couldn't believe that there was someone out there who still cared whether she lived or died. But she had started to become a little guarded with her too.

"I told you... I'll be here with you in your matchbox," Sanya joked.

Ray giggled at the remark. "But hey, it's so peaceful in here."

"Yeah it's peaceful..." She looked around. "But too peaceful isn't good."

"Do you want something to eat?" Ray offered her some fruit salad.

"No, I'm good. I'm here for you. So we'll talk."

"Okay..."

"Tell me, what's wrong?" Sanya looked at her worriedly.

"You already know everything."

"Okay... so you... did you send your resume anywhere?"

"Not yet."

"Okay... did you contact that photographer?"

"What photographer?"

"Oh God, that guy we met in the restaurant."

"Oh. No," she said indifferently.

"Let's call him." Sanya's eyes lit up.

"... I don't think he'll be interested now. It's been a very long time."

"Still, we should try."

"I'm not doing it."

"Oh come on, there's nothing to lose here."

"Okay fine if you insist, but you'll talk."

"Fine, dial the number."

Ray dialed his number.

"Hello..." Sanya was being professionally sweet. Ray didn't know why she smiled.

"Yes?" It was Dev.

"Hi... I'm Sanya. You met me and my friend in the restaurant *some* days ago."

There was a momentary silence.

"Restaurant? Okay." He might have remembered them.

"So, we've called because you had asked us to contact you incase we were interested in doing a body positivity shoot."

"Uh... yes... come to my office tomorrow morning at ten."

"Okay thanks, bye."

"Bye."

"He seemed like he was sleeping," Ray mentioned.

"Why do we care? We're going to be modelling..!"

Sanya instantly started doing her happy dance, clapping and moving her fists in circles. Ray burst out laughing.

"So that means, we're going tomorrow..!" Sanya gathered from Ray's laugh. And then she started dancing even faster, banging her head in the air.

After dinner, Sanya stroked Ray's hair and in a very, very long time, she slept peacefully.

Chapter 37

PERCEPTION

"Hi, we're here to audition," Ray initiated.

"Yes, please be seated there, Mr. Dev will be here soon," the receptionist signaled towards a sofa.

Sanya couldn't help but look around in awe. "I can't believe we're modelling Ray!"

"Ya Sans, but there are no people here other than that receptionist. No models either? I mean he must get swarmed by girls, eager to get their photoshoots done. It's strange, isn't it?"

"Maybe it's because today's Saturday?" Sanya suggested.

Ray and Sanya waited there for an hour before he showed up.

"HellO ladies," he said as soon as he looked at them.

"Hi Dev!" Sanya beamed.

"Hi," said Ray as soon as he looked at her.

"Hope you didn't mind my coming late. Had some preoccupations," he said with his hands in his pockets, standing tall. "I hope you know that it's just an audition, right? The result of your photoshoot will decide whether you will be selected or not. Are we good?"

"Yeah," they both looked at each other and nodded.

"Please come in one by one."

"I'll be the first!" Sanya declared. "You wait outside."

"Okay," Ray smiled at Sanya. Ray sat back on the sofa which was right in front of the reception desk. She kept repositioning herself awkwardly.

At one moment, her and the receptionist's eyes met and they both smiled superficially. She admitted that the receptionist looked like a model herself. She was imagining Sanya being all her chirpy self in front of the camera; she was definitely going to be in the shoot.

As for herself, Ray decided she was going to make it quick for she was growing restless. Suddenly, Sanya opened the door.

"Yeah... definitely. Ya, I've seen that movie. Okay I'll send her in," Sanya chirped looking back at Dev like Ray had imagined.

Ray gave Sanya a sleazy look.

"Go in." Sanya almost pushed her in.

"Sans..." Ray groaned

"Hey, miss..?"

"Ray."

"Yes, miss Ray, please get changed into that white tank top and stand on that spot." He pointed to a cross marked on the green nylon carpet.

Ray came back after changing. They both looked at each other and smiled. Dev kept looking at her face for a little longer.

"You have beautiful hair."

Ray wasn't expecting that. She expected something more like... "and eyes". She felt her cheeks burn.

"I want you to relax... really relax," he said in a hypnotic voice. He put on some music in the background. "It'll help you relax."

A slow, transcendental music with tintinnabulations and binaural beats that came from speakers on both her sides.

"Now, I want you to look at the camera," he said.

She looked straight.

"That's gorgeous. Beautiful." He looked at her with a wan smile.

He clicked four more shots.

"Why do you look sad?"

She was caught off guard. "Oh! I must be sleepy."

"But you still look beautiful."

Ray smiled, "Thanks."

While she posed according to his directions, she found herself looking at him, really looking at him. She saw how focused he was, on his work, on her poses, on **her**.

Her mind was hazy and she liked it. She really noticed his physique for the first time, it was... not bad. But his eyes were vacant just like his smile. He seemed to be escaping from something.

"And that's your final shot." He gave her a thumbs-up and the spell was broken.

"Okay, good, thanks a lot for your time," she said nervously.

"No, don't mention it, it was my pleasure." And he blinked his eyes which seemed sincere. "It was nice meeting you." He reached out for her hand.

"Yes, nice to meet you too."

And Ray left.

***

"You seemed really happy today," Ray teased Sanya.

"He seemed like a nice guy you know, for such a known photographer. I didn't expect to get along with him so well." Sanya's eyes were sparkling.

"Oh really..?"

"Yeah, we talked about movies and food and fashion magazines..."

"Hey watch out!" Ray snapped.

They both sprang up and banged back in their car seats.

"Oops! Didn't see that pit coming." Sanya bit her tongue.

"Sans, easy."

"Yeah, so we talked about many things."

"What else did he talk about?"

"Nothing else." Sanya gave her a short spanning look. "He seemed fun nonetheless. Don't you think?"

"Yeah, me too." But Ray thought he seemed more... more... kind of tragically dark. And she looked at her body as she remembered her photoshoot.

***

"I love you Sans, you're the best." Ray was truly grateful for having her in her life.

"I just want to see you happy. You're my best friend."

"Forever." And Ray hugged her goodbye.

She felt a harmony in her body after such a long time and she didn't want it to go away.

Chapter 38

THE DEVIL

The devil, crawling, asked her again, from a wall behind her, "Are you sure you're Good?"

"Yes," a meek voice said.

"Are you sure?" He was now speaking right in her ear.

She took a deep breath and said, "Yes." in a cracked voice.

"Are you sure!?" *the devil thundered, his body ablaze.*

"Yes!" she screamed out of her lungs and could hear nothing else but her own echo.

"Did he call?" Sanya asked on the phone.

"Nope," Ray said it as if she knew Dev wasn't going to.

"We just have to wait a little more." Sanya was assuring herself more. "Wait, let's check on his website if there's any update?" Sanya beamed.

"Good idea indeed."

"Let's see." Sanya opened her laptop and right on the top of the website were seven girls of different body types and complexions. Right in the center was a confident looking, chubby girl who had acid scars on her face and shoulders. Sanya looked at all of them but couldn't recognize anyone. She looked again and then, recognized one— Ray, who was the seventh girl. She looked again. It was her, definitely and somehow that made Sanya not so glad. She had not recognized Ray at first because she had never thought of her that way. She looked again but there was no likeness of herself. Sanya desperately went in, out and around the website several times but nowhere was to be found her own reflection.

"Nothing?" Ray asked.

"No. Nothing," Sanya said dispirited.

"Don't worry, he'll call us." Ray tried to cheer her up.

"You're here."

"Yeah I'm here, on the phone, with you."

"No I mean, you're here on the website."

"What? You're joking."

"No. See for yourself."

"I don't want to see anything. I know you're lying."

"Fine, don't believe me," Sanya resigned.

"It might be someone else who looks a little like me."

"I'm telling you, see for yourself." Sanya was trying to recover.

Ray sensed some truth in her voice.

"I don't want to see anything. I'm only going to see it if you're there too."

"I'm not in it silly, you are and you don't even want to look at it."

"No, I'm not seeing it if you're not there."

"Okay fine. But you look good and different too, do you think he edits or alters photos in someway?"

Ray felt an ouch but she understood her situation and sympathized, "Yeah, you know photographers these days. Even the biggest celebrities' pictures are edited and enhanced."

Ray realized her reply might have a different effect altogether.

"Yes..." Sanya muttered.

"Yeah..."

"Okay Ray, I have to take a bath, smell of sweat. Worked out too much today."

"O great! You've started to work out. Fine, I'll call you later. Bye."

"Bye."

Ray visited the website and was thrilled to see herself. Yes, it was her but she never really realized how beautiful she was until now. She instantly fell in love with the girl she was looking at. Her perception of herself had changed. She had rediscovered herself, in a way.

She was at loss for words to comprehend how she was feeling but what she felt made her feel beautiful, super confident and sanguine. How strange it was that she looked all those things but still used to feel so washed-out inside.

I never really owned myself. I always knew I was attractive, smart and all the good things a girl can be, but I never owned it, never accepted my own powerful presence. How silly of me for never understanding that. I always admired others but how could I fail to see my own light?

What she was experiencing was surreal and nothing like she had ever felt before. It was self-realization.

That evening, Ray felt a spring in her step. She didn't want to hide her light anymore, she wanted the world to see it. The more she stayed in the room, the smaller the room became. So she decided to call up her long lost friends and a movie plan was laid out. Ray tried calling Sanya too but her phone was switched off. She didn't sleep that night. A euphoria was swarming her being.

She looked at herself again and suddenly, all her favourite dazzling moments came rushing to her.

When she had become the college pageant queen, when she had given that excellent presentation, when she was proposed to by Neil, when a girl from her school complimented her for her oratory skills out of nowhere, when she spoke during the picture perception test. She always knew she was smart but she never herself understood the effect she had on others. And now, finally, she saw. She had stepped into her light and that changed something in her.

Ray wanted to thank Dev.

"Yeah it looks, I mean, I look amazing. You made me look amazing." Ray couldn't hide her appreciation.

"You do look amazing. By the way, did I tell you your voice is velvet," he said warmly.

They started talking more from then on. Ray would feel **seen** again after talking to Dev. It was such a nice break from her mundane state of mind.

First thing in the morning, he would call her to make a plan for the evening. Ray would still think of Neil sometimes but she was hooked on the attention. She felt like it was rightful of her to have a break from all the trauma she was going through. So she entertained him as long as he entertained her. She didn't really trust him. Didn't trust anyone per se. Sis was in it for the feel-good factor.

Ray and Dev started talking every night too which she didn't like because it left her no time to think for her future but she still, was too scared to be alone; to lose company now that even Sanya wasn't talking to her.

Dev left no chance of complimenting her. Sometimes her eyes, other times her lips, her voice and her figure.

Whenever they went out, Dev chose what they were going to eat. It's not like he didn't ask her. He did but nonchalantly and she was okay with anything as long as she had company. That's what she thought.

It used to remind her of Neil who wouldn't stop asking her what she was going to have until she chose something for the both of them.

Sometimes, Dev would click pictures of her, without asking and she would ask him to delete them right away.

"Don't do that again." She would get unsettled.

"Okay, I won't." And he would delete them in front of her.

It was a clear indication from her to him that this was not a real relationship. And he seemed to have no problem with that.

Sanya had stopped calling so Ray tried calling her again. She picked up.

"Hey supermodel, you seem to be doing well. You're so much more popular now. You must feel very lucky." It was the first thing that Sanya said, in one breath.

"Yeah... I'm better Sans, all because of you," Ray said, gulping the tinge.

"Yeah and because of that photographer."

"Oh come on, he's not even a good friend. I don't have any interest in him. I was just wondering how you are, you know we haven't talked in such a long while. Do you want to go somewhere?"

"Okay, let's go to a club, the three of us," Sanya said it. Just like that.

"You want him to come too?"

"Yes, why not?"

Sanya seemed so enthusiastic after such a long time that Ray couldn't refuse. "Okay, we'll go if you want," Ray said hesitantly.

***

As the days went by, Dev was getting more and more comfortable with her. He would try to put his hand on her shoulder and her waist but she would remove it gently.

Sometimes, he asked her to sit closer to him while they were in a restaurant or any public place and if any of his not-so-high-profile friends **somehow** found him hanging out with her, he would show her off to them, "Isn't she ravishing?"

Once, he had kissed her on the hand without her permission and she was stunned at his daring. But again, she didn't want to confront him violently. Instead, she wanted to get rid of him slyly, in a more **ladylike and diplomatic** fashion that minimised the repurcussions. Thenceforth she knew that she had to give up her fear of being alone for her own greater good. But the promise she made to Sanya wasn't to be broken.

"I'm sorry Ray, I can't come," said Sanya.

"But Sans, I agreed to go with him only because you were going to be there too. If you don't go, what will I do there? I don't trust that guy. He might bring other guys with him too. I don't trust him like that you know that."

"I'm sorry Ray, but I really can't come. If you're not comfortable, don't go. Otherwise, do as you please."

"Hold on, he's calling."

"Hey… you ready? I'll be there in five minutes," Dev said authoritatively.

"Hey, actually Sanya isn't coming so—"

"No problem then, you and I will go and there's one more friend of mine."

"Listen, I don't want to go." She was firm.

"Why?"

"I'm not comfortable with you bringing other guys."

"But I've already arranged with him."

"I don't care. I'm not coming." She hung up.

Phone rang again after a few minutes.

"Listen, he's not coming now okay. Now we both can go," he said bitterly.

"No, I don't want to. I'm really tired."

"I'll be there outside your room, your decision whether you want to come or not."

He blared the car horn repeatedly. Irritated, Ray went out.

"I'll come with you only on one condition that we're not going to the club." She made sure he heard her.

"What? that's ridiculous."

"You heard me."

"Fine, get in we're going to a restaurant."

***

They reached the restaurant and he stopped his car. "Get out."

Ray came out abruptly but kept quiet. She didn't want to create a scene in public.

He ordered cheese burgers for the both of them.

"Come on, eat! Hurry up."

"You don't have to talk to me like that."

"I can do a lot of talking without me uttering a word." He gave her a nasty look.

Ray was hoping for it all to end soon so she could go back to her room hopefully. She was really scared of what was going to happen and what was she going to do if something happened to her?

My parents don't care if I'm alive or not anyway. And if something seemed strange, I'll scream and shout.

On the way out, he grabbed her hand and took her to the car forcefully.

"What is this? I'm not going anywhere. I just want to go back to my place."

"Fine, I'm taking you there."

"You better." She didn't show any sign of fear.

They both got into the car.

"Your behavior is just too petty... I'll teach you a lesson. You bitch," he whispered through his teeth.

"What lesson? Stop the car I'm getting out. Right now! I'll go by myself."

"I said, I'm taking you to the fricking room."

"Better."

Ray took out her phone and pretended to talk to someone. She took a breath of relief when she finally saw her street.

"Get out," he said like he was threatening her.

She came out at once and went inside. Ray heard a loud screeching of tires which, eventually, faded away... to her relief.

She couldn't believe she had been treated like that when not a single guy had been able to do that. Ever.

She took a look in the mirror and found herself looking really good.

Do I look inviting? Have I become an attention seeker now?

But she was not going to let any shame and doubt live rent-free in her head. It was time to be strong and she decided to never let him back in her life again. She knew he would call back spinelessly to apologize to her later on. But her parents had raised her for a far better human, not him.

"I used to be a lonely kid, they all thought that I was... even my parents thought I was weird. I had no friends growing up. Man, the world really is a nasty place. Nobody cared about how I felt but I got my revenge. Look how big and famous I'm now," he had said to her on their first meeting. She had sympathy for him then but now, she was utterly disgusted by him.

He might be having his issues but it is not my fricking responsibility to fix him.

Ray wasn't going to let anyone destroy her again. She blocked him from everywhere and forgot about him like a forgotten nightmare.

Chapter 39

THE DEVIL RETURNS

"Hi."

It was the unbelievable happening. Ray couldn't believe what she was witnessing right in front of her eyes. She raised an eyebrow. It was a message from Neil?!

"Tut, tut, tut, look who's back seeing my glow-up."

Ray smiled in pity. She ignored the message. For two days. Then she thought of having some fun. She replied,

"Hi."

"How are you?" he texted back.

"I'm good."

"So what's going on?"

"Nothing."

"Okay... Can I tell you something?"

"Sure."

"You are getting more and more gorgeous with every passing day."

Her cheeks burned red.

"Thanks."

"I always knew you could do great."

"It's just me."

Neil would text her everyday and for a fortnight, she would text him only if she had nothing else to do. She didn't have much to do but her dreams were rekindled. Ray was keen on developing an action plan and taking some solid actions more powerfully than ever before.

Neil never stopped texting her. "If you have time, can we talk?" he asked.

"Not yet. I'll call you, whenever possible," she texted back callously.

Their texts weren't as romantic as they used to be but the chemistry was still there.

Soon, their texting became a daily thing and Ray felt unwanted questions and unresolved emotions rise up in her again. She didn't want him like she used to but still, she wasn't sure if she wanted to go away from him. He was being really tolerant of her bad behaviour.

Maybe, we can put the bad memories aside and start afresh? Maybe it's a sign?

she would wonder every time she went to bed and her **head** counsellor did not like it.

She would go through scenarios in her head where she was with him again and then a question would arise every time she did that:

Will I be able to forgive him? I've seen the worst of my life and he wasn't with me. And now that I'm better, he's back.

She knew what the answer was.

***

"Hi," he texted again.

"Hi."

"How are you?"

"I want to ask you something," Ray said before the conversation escalated.

"Yeah, sure." He listened intently.

"Why are you talking to me? It's not like you're in love with me or something. I'm not even a friend... then why?"

"It's just that I like to spend time with you." He said without thinking twice.

So he doesn't love me.

She hated that she had forgotten that he didn't.

He continued, "I don't know what might happen in the future so I just want to be happy now, in the moment."

The reason why she decided to do the same was that she didn't have anyone else to talk to or that's what she thought. Maybe she hoped to find her old companion, her soul's comfort back after all.

"If you have time, can I call you?"

"Okay."

Ray picked up and "Hello," he said. She heard the deep and a bit playful voice that she loved so much, once again.

She couldn't help but smile. All her doubts flew away like birds fly away from power lines. And she was again the happiest girl in the world.

"Hello," she replied. Something told her that he felt the same way about her.

"Your voice..." he said, "It's still different, from everyone else's."

"Thanks." She meant it.

They talked about their lives in general, their families, politics and random things. They would share some posts and memes with each other. This went on for a few days before Ray started to get restless. Things between them were not going the way she had hoped to.

There was still an invisible wall that the two couldn't get through, or he didn't want to go through. Where was this relationship going now? Is there a future? She felt that the late-night calls were taking too much of her time and energy but she wasn't getting anything **real** in return. No sign that could mean that he wanted to take things forward. He only seemed to be interested in the superficial surface stuff and it seemed like he was talking to her only to take a break from work.

She was no more the type to speak and speak without actually talking to someone. Experience had become her. She felt uneasy, taken for granted and the last thing that she wanted to feel was being used.

"I don't think I want to talk to you anymore," she said with a huge lump in her throat.

"May I know why?" He was calm and collected.

"Because I can pass time with anyone, but not with you. I can't just pretend that you weren't anything to me. And it hurts to see us this way. I'd rather live without you than be like this."

"Talking to me doesn't make you happy?"

Ray went silent. It did make her happy. In fact, her love for him was the only thing that felt anything like happiness.

"It does, but I can't keep talking to you like this unless I can see something well-founded with you."

"...You already know how we could be together."

She remembered the time when he had told her that he wanted a fiercely ambitious woman as his better-half. Someone, who would be able to face all troubles, trials and tribulations herself. And she knew, she wasn't that person right now. She was no hero. Ray just never understood why someone would put conditions on love.

Wasn't being together enough for him?

She knew it wasn't. Ray couldn't help but wonder why it was not enough for him when it was everything she wanted?

"I remember what you're talking about, but I can't become something just because someone else or you want me to."

She knew it was the truth but a truth he didn't want to listen. Ray didn't care because she never asked him of anything in return. She never asked him to change.

"It's all up to you. I'm happy anyway," he said.

***

"So, that means you guys are together? Again?" asked Sanya overenthusiastically. Although she had started talking to Ray again, her tone always seemed a bit off.

"Oh, no. He just texted me one day and I barely respond to him," said Ray, trying not to get Sanya's hopes high and even her own.

"He was a great guy you know. What's he doing these days?"

"He's about to be promoted to... I don't know which profile, didn't bother to ask."

"That's great... I'm so happy for you."

"Sans, I don't think of him that way anymore."

"But he's a nice guy, you know there were so many girls after him but he chose you."

On hearing that, Ray couldn't help but reminisce about the time gone-by. "Those were different times," she said nostalgically.

"I'm going to call him and congratulate him. I'm so happy."

"Do you, but I don't see him that way."

"But what if he does? I'll find out everything. After all, he's like my brother."

Ray felt that it was a little unnecessary to mention.

"I know, you don't have to mention that Sans. Okay, got to go for dinner. See you soon."

Chapter 40

A VEIL WILL BE LIFTED

"You got your nails done? That's something new," Neil said.

"Wait, did I tell you that?"

"You know."

"I didn't... no I didn't tell you... but I told Sanya. Oh, so she told you haan?"

"Maybe."

"Yeah, she did. So what else did you guys talk about other than me." Ray couldn't help but feel uneasy.

"Her last call to me was two days ago and that too for five minutes. So you can guess how much conversation took place between the two of us."

"Your last call to her was today," she mentioned off the bat.

"I didn't have enough time to talk. I was busy."

"Okay." Ray tried to let it go because again, she didn't want to lose her ease.

Ray would call Sanya only to find the line busy most of the times. Her time to talk to Neil was fixed, everyday after dinner.

A month went on and Neil seemed to grow distant from her.

How long could we go on like that anyway,

she comforted herself.

He didn't text her today and she didn't want to care but still couldn't help asking him.

"Everything okay?"

"Yes, why?" he replied.

"You didn't text."

"Ya. I was busy."

"When aren't you?" No one responded. She continued, "Did I... say anything not right? If there's anything like that you can tell me. I won't disturb you again."

"No, you haven't done anything. Uh... I got to go. Bye."

Neil didn't call her back that day, not the next day and not for two more days.

At least Sanya got the time to call her back.

Ray was happy nonetheless. "Hi... where have you been. Did you get a new boyfriend or something and forgot about your best friend? I called you so many times!" she teased.

"Nothing, I have been so busy these days... by the way, congratulations to Neil."

"Why?"

"He didn't tell you? He has been given a raise. He told me when I called him last night."

Ray's heart sank.

Neil hadn't even bothered to return her texts and he picked up Sanya's call?

"That's great," she said, pretending to be okay.

"Why... he didn't tell you?" Sanya was quick to ask.

"No, I haven't been talking to him." Ray's voice lost all expression.

"I see, but why? I thought you two had started talking again."

"Yes we did. Not anymore."

"Don't worry. I'll ask him to talk to you. I'll make him understand. Don't worry."

"Thanks Sans, I'll see you later."

She wasn't going to. Ray had understood everything— why Neil had become distant again and why Sanya's been too busy to attend her calls. Neither she wanted to know anything anymore nor did she want any explanation. It was futile. Ray had no time to think or feel despair. She was fed up with sorrow and was surprised with her own reaction. The next moment, she knew what she had to do.

"I won't be standing between you two anymore. Never was I ever doing that. I will never come between my ex and my ex best friend. All the best for the future."

And that was her last message to Neil. She didn't know why she felt exhilarated. Like a bird inside her had remembered that it had wings.

Every relationship that she had ever leaned on had vanished into thin air. She had nothing to lose.

Despite everything, I'm still here. I'm alive. I made it through the worst of my times and now sorrow doesn't budge me anymore like it used to. I'm still here even after everything and everyone is gone.

She went to look at herself in the mirror to see if her face showed any sadness. But it looked anew. Ray couldn't help but smile the widest and brightest smile. Her chest felt open. She had freed herself. Ray had found herself.

It was another self-realization, but this time, it was deeper.

Ray was thankful that God took away the drama. She loved the fact that she had all of her focus on herself now.

I want to love this person in the mirror who has stood by me through everything. I want to love me more than I've ever loved anyone else.

She felt like the light bulb went dim, the streetlight was dimmer, the light of the moon and the stars looked awestruck because the brightest light in the moment was her own.

Ray decided to not dwell in the past. She decided to remember the lessons. And most importantly, she decided to be happy **for no reason at all.**

I was sad for such futile and volatile things. Things that were never meant to stay. Now, I will be happy for this one, the one who stayed.

She immediately opened her drawer looking for something. Ray grabbed it and went to the dustbin outside. She didn't even wait to look after throwing it in. It was her medication.

Don't need any pills to keep me numb from my happiness. I'll give myself time and love. I will heal myself with the same care I gave to others. I'll be patient with me and I'll embrace what's good for me. Forever. And those pills were good for nothing! I'm going to learn to be happy. I'll tell myself that being not okay isn't okay anymore. Being okay is okay. And I'll channel all my self discipline into teaching myself to be okay. No matter what.

"Ray is a happy girl. Ray is free."

Chapter 41

PURPOSE

Tearing through the silent darkness, came out a fizzing, too big a moon. It came from the left of her eye with a fizzy sound that almost pierced her eardrums. As the super moon rose, it became brighter and brighter, the sound fizzier and fizzier and when her closed eyes couldn't bear the brighter-than-the-sun light, she opened her eyes wide.

She looked out of her window and the wind was dancing gracefully with the trees and birds. The sky had blanketed the city with dark clouds. Winter was near.

"I love winter, the cold."

So much so that she bathed in cold water in winter. Almost each one of her friends seemed to like the summers more. She hated it. The sweat, the harsh sun, the heat; made her head feel like that static on television.

"Let's get started, Ray."

She had been planning to start something of her own right back from her college days.

Unlike her early kindergarten days when kids used to ask each other who they wanted to become and she used say that she wanted to pursue all the professions that she knew about back then— A scientist, a joker, a sweeper man; not a woman but a man, a teacher, a dancer, and the list went on.

She couldn't help but laugh, "Silly kid, she didn't know that she was someone already. I am someone already. No more trying to become something that I'm not."

With that knowing, she revisited her college idea, The Third Eye, which was a tracker cum camera that was installed in a hair clip. So if a woman wearing the device on the back of her head was being followed or she had any red flags showing up, she would press the power button on her phone twice which will turn on the device which was also connected to an application on her phone.

Simultaneously, her live location and real time video from the camera will be sent to the nearest police station and her relatives.

She so badly wanted to make that idea a reality back then but it required a lot of coding for the app and it wasn't her specialization.

She had reached out to a couple of college seniors who had the competence to write the code for the application but they were already busy with their final year projects. Ray had even thought of paying them some cash in return of their time and specialization but she didn't have the money back then.

Ray had even decided to take up a part time job at a fast food outlet on weekends and she had even gotten the opportunity to work there but she had to leave the idea because of her own college syllabus was humungous along with the assignments and projects. She couldn't make time to do it all on weekdays.

So both time and money were issues back then. But now, she had all the time in the world for herself, enough skill and opportunities to make money.

But she didn't want to go with that right now. She would make the product and market it after she had made a substantial sum of money and that was going to take time. So she had to look for something simpler. Something she knew very well. Something that would give her a sense of purpose and not just a blind chase for money. She had heard somewhere that in order to make millions, you have to touch millions of people's lives in whatever or whichever way possible. Ray knew all that but what it was going to be, she still did not know. So she decided to keep on searching and looking for it until she finds a thread to follow.

She was thinking and thinking and a thought occurred to her,

What if Déjà vu is like, my higher self in the future, in a future situation and then as time passes, I actually see the same situation again and Déjà vu occurs?

A strange musing but she was amazed at her own thoughts. And a moment later, something clicked.

Alright, that's what I'm going to do. I'm going to do something that I know very well and that something should be rare so that people are interested. Like a USP of my service. Did I just think service? So I'm providing a service, mm, okay.

But what's a rare service? Okay, so what is one thing that I don't have?

Lovely relationships.

Yes! That's the only thing I don't have. Like, people run into trouble because of other people all the time

and sometimes all they need is a friend to talk to who won't bitch behind their backs and someone who'd keep their secrets. You know, like a counsellor but this will be cheaper than a counsellor.

Ray smiled wickedly. She was amazed by her own intellect.

"I'm so smart man, can never imagine why I was so sad before. I'm too fly to be sad."

To her, it felt like ages had passed since she last felt so alive. Yes, she was doing better and felt happy but something about this feeling was different from all of that. No doubt, being happy and positive was the way to live but somehow, she felt like there was no life without this feeling she didn't know the name of. But it touched the deepest ends of her in a way that nothing ever could and because of that, she knew that it was the right thing to do, that she was on the right path.

Chapter 42

CONFIDANTE

Ray opened her social media and made a page immediately. It was called 'COMPANIONS' and the page description went like this:

Let it out! Yes, let it out!

In these fast pacing and racing times, our emotions get left out in the dust more than often.

We believe your mental health is as important as your physical health.

Sometimes, all you want is a COMPANION who can listen to you without any judgements.

That's why we created a supportive professional environment where you can be contacted by one of our executives and be listened to without any judgements with just a meagre amount of 500 INR for 30 minutes only!

We hope to hear from you.

****DISCLAIMER****

× We do not share your identity with anyone.

× No explicit content will be entertained.

× Age no bar.

Drop a direct message and be contacted by one of our executives.

We look forward to serve you soon.

She shared the post online but with a fake id. Ray would not let anyone be thinking that she was running a cheap call center. First, she just wanted to run a good experiment without fearing any judgements. So she decided to use a different name while dealing with a client.

Everyday, she would wake up and share the post everywhere. In addition to that, she had posted new ones with some pictures and illustrations of people helping each other.

That's what she wanted to do, helping people. The idea was to have enough presence online that clients will feel safe contacting her. And if anyone reached out to her, she will ask them to share their feedback on their social media. And once she starts getting a steady revenue, she will start hiring psychiatrists too! She had it all laid out in her mind-estate.

Two days went by and nothing happened. No clients, no messages.

Maybe I should decrease the fee.

She brought it down to 300 INR for one hour. Another two days went by but nothing happened.

"I need people to testify that it works. Fine."

She reached out to two of her neighbors and promised to take them out for a meal, if they wrote and spoke highly of her service on social media and kept her identity private.

Ray also asked two guys from her college to do the same. She had once helped them with their final year presentations. They agreed and didn't even want any favours in return.

"You can throw us a huge party when you get rich," they said.

"Ha-ha, that's a given."

***

Tuturu! A notification.

~ 174 ~

She picked up her phone hoping to see something good and good for her expectation, she did see something good. A message from someone named Antim with no profile picture.

"Hello."

"Hello Sir, this is Menka how may I help you today?"

"Are you guys professionals? Like, do you have any psychiatrists or counsellors helping you?"

"Sir, to be honest with you, we are here to make you feel heard and we do not provide any professional counsel. We're only here to make you feel like you have someone to talk to. Your privacy is our biggest priority. So sir, how may I help you today?"

"And how much do you charge for your service?"

"It's usually 300 INR for an hour of conversation but today's special offer is 250 for an hour."

"I see."

"Would you like to start the conversation, sir?"

Nobody replied. She got tired of waiting and put the phone aside.

"Am I still charging too much? Whatever, if it works, it works, if it doesn't, it doesn't."

She went on to chew on some walnuts.

Tuturu!

"Hello Miss poppy123, how may I help you today?"

"How much do you charge?" texted Miss poppy123.

"Only 150 INR for an hour. It's a special offer for today."

"Okay."

"So miss Poppy, is there anything you would like to talk about? Shall we start with your interests, your hobbies?"

"Okay."

"What are your hobbies, miss?"

"Cooking."

"That's very creative."

It took a very long chase to get to the point.

"So miss Poppy, is anything bothering you?"

"Yes."

"What is it?"

"I have an exam tomorrow and haven't studied anything."

"Well, miss Poppy exams can seem very tough but we can start with the easiest chapters."

"I see. That's a good idea, but i don't feel like studying."

Seriously?!

"You must. It's a way of ensuring a brighter future."

"Brighter future my jackass, I want to make music."

"Then you should tell your parents."

"I don't have any parents."

"I'm very sorry. Then who's your guardian?"

"My elder brother."

"Then you should let him know about your aspirations."

"I did, but he thinks I'm not serious. Why? Because I wear tattoos? And piercings? That corporate worm could never. What does he know about creative expression?"

"I urge you to keep the conversation appropriate, miss. I do think that you are his responsibility and he's your brother, you must let him know that you can be serious."

"And how do I do that?"

"By getting good grades. That's a way to show him that you can actually focus on something and achieve it."

"I guess. Thanks. Didn't have anybody else to talk to."

"I'm very happy to have helped you miss. It's been 30 minutes and that will be 75 INR for half an hour."

"I've already sent it."

Ray checked her phone. It was there.

"Thank you very much for your payment. All the very best for your exam."

Ray couldn't believe she had gotten her first payment just like that! It wasn't much of a hassle.

"Oh God! I didn't tell her to share a feedback on social media. I'll remind her tomorrow. Anyways, I know she'll be like, 'Yeah sure, I'll share it but it's not like anyone is interested in my stuff.'"

Ray was jumping in excitement, even though she could only buy herself her favorite chocolate with that money, she was the happiest girl in the world.

She felt a sense of purpose knowing that she had helped someone through a tough time even though nobody was there for her.

That's exactly why I'm so happy. I know that feeling and now I'm helping people having that same feeling. No better way to make money than to actually help someone in return.

She decided to go with the new decreased service fee for other clients from then on.

Tuturu!

It was Mr. Antim with no profile picture at 8 p.m. Ray was about to start her dinner.

But okay, let's do this for the innumerable fancy dinners in the future.

Yeah, but nothing can beat the simple roti and veggies.

Ray smiled after realizing the truth in that.

"Welcome back sir, how may I help you?"

"Uh... nothing. I just. Okay, I have something to share but you say you won't share it with anyone else?"

"That's right sir, your privacy is our biggest concern."

And mine too. LOL.

"What's your name?"

"Menka, sir."

"Okay, so I have this girl that I have a crush on. She's like, the most beautiful person I have ever seen and she spends a lot of time with me too. But."

"Yes."

"But... she's... Out of nowhere, she told me about this another guy who she had a crush on and he accepted her proposal too."

"That's good news for her."

"Yes, I know but I can't help but feel left out in the dust. Like, how did she spend so much time with me if she already had eyes for someone."

"Did you ever let her know about your feelings for her?"

"Unfortunately, no. But she always seemed so happy with me that I thought..."

"She must have considered you as a friend." But Ray doubted so.

"I don't know but I'm so heartbroken that I can't forget her. How do I even try to live."

"I'm sure you will find someone better, sir."

"Let's hope so."

"You should definitely move on with your life sir, and make your dreams come true then there will never be a lack of suitors for you."

"Yes, you're right. I will try."

"You will succeed, sir."

"Thank you."

"Thank you very much for the payment sir, if I could help you in anyway, please share our page on your social media."

"Definitely, I will, as soon as I get time. Anyway, can I get your personal number?"

"It's against our policy. I'm very sorry, sir."

Ray was growing fond of the stories, narratives and accounts that she was finding through her clients.

Few were repetitive— Someone broke someone's heart. But most of them were so different from anything that she had witnessed in her own life.

Yes, money was a reward but to see someone really open up their heart was something she had rarely seen happen.

She realized how the world was connected so much and that too so instantly yet, only some had a real connection with another soul.

She found out that even though her own sorrow had been great, there were more people just like her who ached silently, who had bad things done to them and they still thought twice before hurting or blaming anyone for their suffering. She saw the good in the world for the first time. And because she had completely managed to pull herself out of her own misery, she was happy that she was doing that for others now.

Chapter 43

ESCAPE VELOCITY

Sitting in a damp, dark and murky place, I look at the stars glittering at me from my lap, for they've now become a part of my dress.

One time, a grandpa messaged Ray saying he missed his kids and grandkids.

Another time, a housewife who was a victim of domestic violence contacted her. Ray managed to convince her to talk to a women's helpline.

There was another client of hers who was a mother who had unfortunately, lost her child. Ray could never imagine in her wildest dreams that there could be so many people reaching out to her to tell their stories.

It was time to create a workforce and a guideline too so that her employees could be sympathetic enough and yet professional with their clients. She hired a junior from her college who was ready to work part-time.

Six months later, she had seven people working under her leadership. One year later, she had more than enough resources to afford herself a life that no one in her circle had imagined. She was already making more money than her peers would be able to make in years.

She remembered her tough times. The time when someone had told her that she would regret leaving, that she would be sorry and would not find work. She remembered that time too when someone had told her that she was not special when she was at her lowest ebb. Now, she had proved them all wrong. **She had won**. Bigger than all of them and she was going to be bigger than they will ever be. She felt her power running in her veins and steaming out from her body.

***

"We're so proud of you Ray, the designer saree that you bought me, everyone was in awe of it. They loved it. They all said that your hard work on your daughter has paid off."

"Hard work indeed, LOL." Ray couldn't help but make that remark.

Her mother reached for her and held her in her arms. Ray could smell that familiar scent and she, too, put her hands on her mother's waist gently. She was happy in that moment. There was no use clinging to the baggage. But she still didn't trust anyone to the fullest.

"I knew it'd look great on you," Ray said, smiling as best as she could.

She looked at her old bedroom door, it was open. Ray went inside to find her father sitting on her bed with his head down. "Dad." She was concerned.

He didn't look up.

"Dad, I brought you something. Please try it." Her voice cracked and eyes, wet; a little red.

She went in there to sit beside him.

"Dad, look." It was a wristwatch, platinum. Her father looked at it once and a tear rolled down his cheek.

"Dad, don't cry, please."

"When did my daughter grow up so much?" He still didn't look up.

Ray couldn't help herself anymore. She started weeping and it felt like a burden of a lifetime was lifted. Her parents didn't think she was a burden anymore.

"I wasn't a good father. I know."

"No dad I... I wasn't a—"

"Don't lie. I could never understand that the Almighty had sent me the biggest blessing of my life as you."

"Dad..."

"You've done something I could've never been able to do. You've outgrown your dad."

"No dad, you're still my dad and not the other way around."

Ray's father broke into a weak laughter. Ray knew she was experiencing a miracle and she captured it in her heart for forever.

"Dad, try this." She held his hand in hers and he kept looking at her trying to lock the wristwatch in place.

"Dad... I don't know how this works, you do it."

And he clicked the watch into place at once. "I'm proud of you."

Chapter 44

MONEY, POWER, GLORY AND A CONSTANT LIGHTNING

Two years later...

Hey look, there's a thunderstorm developing there. Ray pointed at the humungous formation of white-black clouds over the ocean. The formation looked like a huge terrifying bear's mouth was open and it would gulp down anything that even dared to look at it. Ray kept looking at it. She knew what she was thinking and she had to stop her. But she had already run into that direction. A great lightning whiplashed the ocean to its bed and spread out in the bare ocean. She now heard an august cathedral music roaring in the skies. She went closer and closer, the lightning stood there, raging, constant, like the thunderclouds had to get rid of the godly rage in them without taking a breath. And she saw its blinding power in front of her, just a nose away. She stepped into the constant current and felt it go through her. Ray watched her from afar. She stretched her arms out and she was lit up. The current made her brighter and brighter until the light exploded out, blinding Ray's vision.

She opened up her eyes thinking she might have touched a live wire somehow. But there was nothing.

She was listed in the The Pros magazine as the youngest woman entrepreneur of the year. Her college idea had apparently helped hundreds of thousands of women around the world.

Ray was sitting in her bungalow's balcony as she looked at her image in the magazine that the world was seeing.

She didn't go for the cliché look of arms crossed, a proud smile and a sharply cut suit. Instead, she was smiling her best smile and flashing the victory fingers. She had her hair a little messy, she wore her old-yet-gold purple T-shirt and blue jeans that always worked which her dad and mom had bought her when she was sixteen. Her interviewer was clueless about how it still fit her.

"I was always very disciplined when it came to diet," Ray let her know.

She had given a speech in front of ten thousand people. It went like this,

"Thank you for your time that you've saved to listen to me today.

I don't want to list out my struggles today and the reason for that, is that there's not a single person in this world who doesn't have a fair share of their struggles.

There are people out there who have struggled more than I did so I won't be glorifying suffering. I will be glorifying the power of choice though.

That's the most powerful thing we have.

When people doubted me and said, 'You're no special. You're going to regret this,'

I chose to write my own destiny.

When people played me for a fool, I chose to forgive them and be more discerning in the future.

When I, myself thought that I was weak, I chose to make myself see the brighter side. I always tried, at least.

Because you can never be too harsh on yourself.

You learn with Love and Self-Discipline.

I chose to be kind and accepting because the world seemed to be in utter lack of those virtues.

That's what I urge people to do.

Let's change the notion that kindness is a weakness.

Let's make the world see the truth that kindness is actually a trait of the strongest of characters.

Let's love more and accept more.

Thank you very much."

There was a pin drop silence for a second and then, there were showers of applaud, roaring of claps. She stood still to take it all in. Trying to not let her tears out. Instead, she smiled her brightest smile and joined her hands in gratitude, "Thank you."

***

It was raining outside and she watched the sky strike translucent flashes of green. Ray was trying to capture the blue-green colour and the luminous clouds and bring it onto her sketch. So she waited for the flashes of lightning to strike in order to really notice their colour and then mimic it onto her canvas.

"So beautiful," her mother said.

Ray smiled a little, "No, it's not done yet."

"I wasn't talking about the sketch."

"Mom, I know what you're going to say."

"You have everything now dear, wouldn't it be great to have someone to share it all with?"

"Mom, I don't know if there's someone out there for me." She paused a little. "You know, there are many guys who are only interested in the shimmer. They will say they like my ambition. But that's all they're interested in. They want this ideal image of me." She pointed at her magazine cover.

"... And not the real me. If there's someone out there who'll be there for me no matter what, who will want my pain too and who won't judge me if I lost it all tomorrow then I don't know where he is. I've never met anyone like that. I need someone who understands my journey, you know. Someone who's madly successful but not mad with ambition. There has to be a humility about him. And I haven't found anyone like that." Ray stopped, thinking she might have said too much in vain.

"You think too much. God has definitely made a match for you, you just wait. My heart says he'll come soon."

Ray's phone beeped.

"Hi."

Who's this now?

She tapped on the notification and Déjà vu! It was a message from Neil.

My heart says he'll come soon...

Her mother's words rang in her ears.

"Yes?" she texted back.

"Hi, it's me. I don't know if you remember me. But I'm really proud of you."

"I do remember you and thank you but you don't have a right to be proud of me."

"Okay."

He never dared to love bomb her again.

Ray couldn't stop some old feelings from rising. A tear rolled out easily.

I loved you so much Neil, I was ready to be everything and do everything for you. Why did you do this to us?

She felt like the last of her tears had been exhausted. Now, being over him, she looked at her sketch again.

So beautiful.

And continued with it.

Chapter 45

JUST SOME SOUL STUFF

Ray had joined a mindfulness program that she used to attend on the weekends. Her mother would accompany her upon her constant insisting. But not today.

"You go today, I have a lot of work to do," her mother said, lying on the couch.

"What work is more important than taking care of yourself?" Ray rebelled.

"I have to go help our neighbor's daughter-in-law with my secret pumpkin recipe. She was insisting so much."

"And I'm not? Fine, I'm going."

Ray reached there and her driver parked her custom matte gold Sedan. She paced towards the door that led to a huge hall. Still thinking of why her mother went to the neighbors and now she had no company.

They're always playing earthquaking rash music. Recipe is an excuse, they just want to know our family secrets.

Ray suddenly looked up and took a step back. She had almost run into a guy. He smiled at her understandably and she smiled back slightly, with a foolish face; one eyebrow up, other down and eyes about to come out.

He looked like a well-off gentleman. She dropped her head and went inside without wasting any time.

Oh great! That guy must be thinking like, 'Yeah... this girl totally needs some good meditational peace.'

Ray went in to sit on her usual spot and closed her eyes.

Why is my body and mind so restless today? I haven't felt like this in a long time. No, I can't afford to have an anxiety attack right now. No. Please don't. Why? Why today? Because mom decided to not to come? Am I that upset with that? Or is it something else? Okay, no more questions. Only focus on Guru Ji's voice.

Ray felt peaceful for a moment and then,

I want to open my eyes. I don't want to sit. I want to go outside and run to my car.

Social anxiety? Is it? Ugh. I thought I left all these things in the past. Nooo. Why?!

I know why. Since the day I installed that new social media app, I've been feeling like everyone is looking at me. I feel so uncomfortable.

Ugh! does that mean I can't even use an app that everyone is using? I'm sure there is no death threat there.

What if someone morphed my pictures?

Ray don't fear, don't fear. I'm brave, I'm brave.

"... And... open your... eyes slowly. We thank the Almighty for giving us his blessings and pure energy. Om Shanti."

"Om Shanti," everyone repeated.

Ray let out a deep sigh. She looked to her left and it was the same gentleman. Suddenly, she was conscious of her posture which was perfect anyway though.

Ray came back home and still had that near-miss running in her head.

"It was just an accident. Forget about it."

But she was having a hard time forgetting that smile. She was lying on her bed and closed her eyes.

And remembered that innocent looking face. His jet black hair were a little undone and fell on his forehead here and there. His eyes were black, kind and young, as if holding back the world's unfairness but still believing. His face, a resolve. His eyebrows were perfect and followed the arch of his powerful eyes obediently. Even though, his face was like that of a teenager, something about his slim and tall built suggested he was older, maybe in his late twenties? There was no telling. His cheeks had a slight chubbiness preserved (maybe the reason why his smile was so beautiful), maybe that's why he wore a straight moustache perfectly lined up with his upper lip so that he looked not so young. A little beard around his jawline too. His mouth was small which made his upper smiling curve straighter and his lower lip seemed like filled with pomegranate juice. His complexion, fair, warm and clear.

Damn it! I have acne... But why am I even comparing?!

Ray wanted to know who he was, what he was like.

Wow, Ray. You are thinking about someone you randomly ran into. He just smiled in pity at you and you're taking it that way? Geez, grow up.

Yeah right.

Ray let it go and went to sleep hoping that the next day, she might see him again.

Chapter 46

ER...

The next day, Ray got ready a little extra, her hair in a ponytail, very unusual of her. She wore a ponytail like, once in a year.

"Ugh! Just lose it! Why am I getting so dolled up."

She pulled her hair out of the rubber band and gave it a nice swing so it landed in perfect shape.

"Let's go now."

Ray sat on her usual spot and he was on her left just like the day before but she couldn't care less and tried to act normal by giving a little more attitude. The meditation went just fine and she held her mat and went to her car without taking a single glance at him. Sitting in her car, she felt bad.

I won't be seeing him until the next weekend. I should've given him a hint at least.

Ray was feeling sad and she let herself feel that. His face still haunted her at bedtime.

Time to get really busy now.

The following week, she went on with her meetings, travels, lectures and motivational speeches.

You know what? Life is good like this. I'm not marrying anyone, ever!

And then came Saturday .

"Mom, are you coming?"

"No dear, I told you, didn't I?"

"Yeah I know, your neighbor and your recipe. Yeah I get it. Bye."

"You should take your fa—"

"He's doing fine. Bye"

Great, will have to see him again and I'm alone!? I hope he brings a girl with her so that I can drop the very idea of him.

***

Ray went inside and saw that he had taken her spot. Ray felt bad. And good. She walked confidently and stopped for a split second to act surprised. After all, her spot was taken! She sat on his left with a fake fiery face which he definitely had noticed. She closed her eyes and didn't meditate at all. Didn't even try to! Instead, she was enjoying the smell that was coming from him.

Le Tout-Puissant is it? Extra expensive... but it comes with a female variant too, right? To be worn by couples, isn't it so? So that means he has a girlfriend. YAY! I mean... yay... Now I can meditate in peace.

A few minutes later...

"Om Shanti..." Ray stood up to leave without any adieu.

"Uh... hey!"

Ray looked back at once, "Yes?" with a zero face.

"I'm sorry, I took your spot today."

"Oh that's nothing, you can have that spot." And she turned to leave.

"Uh wait, if I'm not wrong, you're Rayveena, right?"

Ray nodded with a smile.

"Hi, I'm Madhav." He extended his hand

"Hi Madhav." She took it.

"It's very rare to see people our age, visiting meditation centers."

"Yes, that's true they'd rather go to gyms or cafés unless their lives aren't bothersome."

"Ha-ha I have no worries, I'm only here for the experience of it. And there are so many benefits to it."

Ray felt like he was talking too much being a complete stranger. "Yeah sure, um... my driver is waiting, I will have to go."

"Sure, no problem. Take care."

"Sure."

Chapter 47

MR. DASHING

Ray couldn't help but feel bad.

He clearly made a move. Ugh! why didn't I just... damn it.

She looked in the mirror.

What else did you want to do? Look easy? Come on, you can't be too interested in a person, just like that, right?

Ray puckered her lips and went to bed.

The next week was a no-show by him.

"What are you looking for?" her mother asked. She had finally agreed to accompany her daughter after so long.

"Your daughter's future groom," Ray said grimly.

"What? Where?" Her mother ran eyes across the room.

"Mom, I'm joking. I was just looking for Guru Ji. Have to ask him something."

" What about?"

"About... my mind! It's very restless these days."

"Oh."

When they were leaving, Ray saw a black-green luxury coupe in all its might. Her mother didn't seem to notice at all. As they were getting in their car, Ray saw a man in a navy blue double-breasted suit coming out of the coupe. He was wearing some ultra-stylish black aviators and his hair, slicked back.

He was gleaming in the morning sunlight as he looked at the sun and then checked the time on his wrist. Ray had seen many guys of every kind in her life but never had she seen a guy so elegant. He looked so godlike as he breathed in the fresh air. His suit gave a sheer green shine when he moved.

He's matching his clothing with the car? I'm dead. But he looks so... How's that even possible?

The guy looked back at his car and someone else came out too. Maybe his father? Looked so. Definitely.

"No way, no way," Ray said aloud in her car.

"What?" her mom asked, irritated.

"That's the founder of Gold Cups Inc. What's he doing here?"

Her mom peered through the window with her and said, "He's old. Must be here trying to attain nirvana."

The old man was walking heavily and with difficulty. He was using a walking stick but the young man was supporting his drooping shoulders.

"Madhav..." Ray whispered through her lips.

***

Madhav is business tycoon Mr. Chandrashekhar's son!? No way. If he is, why would he approach me? How did he know my name? Magazines... right. Rich people like to make networks for sure. (I don't!). So that must be the reason. He just wanted to make a connection probably.

Ray relaxed and waited for the next day.

Madhav was there on his original spot and Ray sat on his right. She didn't ask her mom to come with her. Instead, told her to teach dad some meditation.

"Hi Mr. Madhav, back to your old spot?"

"Hi Miss Rayveena, yes I'm," he confirmed.

After the meditation, they stood up. Ray looked at him and he looked at her.

"I'm sorry, I left the conversation hanging yesterday, actually I had to take my mom to the doctor," she said.

Why do I lie so smoothly?

"Oh yeah, I saw her yesterday. Is she okay?"

So he saw her?

"It was nothing. Just a regular checkup. She needs a lot of insisting."

At least that's true.

She continued, "I think I didn't see you here yesterday, so how did you see me?"

"Yeah I didn't attend the meditation but I brought my dad here and I guess I saw you guys leaving. Yours is the golden one, right?"

"Yeah right. So he's interested in meditation too. That's great."

Madhav chuckled and Ray cherished.

"No actually, you know, Guru Ji is an astrologer too so dad's interested in that. I brought dad here to meet him. He comes here like, twice a year."

"And do you believe in astrology?"

"Uh... I'm more of a believer of we-make-our-own-destiny. And I guess, belief in astrology has somehow served my dad's destiny."

"Yes, I do feel that we're the masters of our own fate. But my mom is so into astrology." Ray noticed a lot of people were noticing them.

"Let me walk you to your car," Madhav said, noticing the concern on her face.

"Sure. By the way, how did you know my name?" She couldn't help but ask.

"Everyone knows your name these days," he threatened.

Ray looked at him waiting for a more solid answer. Madhav chuckled and Ray cherished.

"Don't worry, I saw you in the magazine like the others did," he said laughingly.

"Oh I see. But you didn't tell me about yourself."

"Well, I'm only a newly appointed chairman of the board of directors of our company."

"You mean CEO."

"Smart. Yes you can say that. I guess this is your car."

"Yep, it is," she said proudly.

Madhav's face looked confused. Ray looked at him questioningly.

"Can I hope to see you next week?" he asked.

Ray was surprised and not surprised. "Most probably."

Chapter 48

A LESSON OF BELIEF

Ray fell asleep quite easily but was suddenly woken up by a nightmare. She thought she saw someone beside her bed. It was a rather tall figure in an orange shawl and turban. She sat up and suddenly remembered who he was. It was Swami Ji from her very early childhood, when she was just a little girl.

Ray and her family used to go to Swami Ji's center every Saturday. Her parents were their avid followers among hundreds of thousands of others all around the world. Ray remembered his teachings. He used to say things like:

"The world is Maya, illusion. It's all momentary, a play rather, to trap you in. Each year, you think you celebrate your kid's birthday? Hah no, child. You're actually celebrating the fact that your kid has stepped one year closer to his death."

Ray's family revered Swami Ji, so much so that they insisted that Ray should do the same. And Ray, an innocent kid, abided. She accepted Swami Ji's grim and dull world view.

"...Your parents aren't your parents, really. The Almighty is. Every relationship, they will all break your trust one by one."

Ray remembered that she used to reiterate the same things to her school friends and boy, were they angry with her declarations. She remembered how her friends had stopped talking to her.

What if it had affected me subconsciously? Was it the start of me becoming isolated? Is that where all my issues started? Is that why I was so angry at the world?

Swami Ji had given his followers the sacred mantras.

"These mantras will protect you. Meditate on them and all your pains will be mine," he used to tell his followers.

Ray used to meditate on those mantras by heart.

"But beware, anyone who dares to tell these mantras to anyone without permission, he or she will have to burn in hellfire."

Ray remembered that as a kid, when her friends were sharing ghost stories with each other, a particular boy that she used to like, got scared and she told him the sacred mantras to ease his fear. But she had committed a sin and now she had to go to hell. That little kid of three was sure she was going there after her death. She was scared to her core but nothing could be done now. So she accepted whatever the punishment might be and became a fearful child.

What the frick? How could've it not affected me? Given the circumstances around me in those days. I was just a kid. My God! Not even my psychiatrist would've been able to go so deep in my past, in my psyche.

Tears welled up in her eyes.

I trusted Swami Ji way too much because I wanted an escape. So I made him my everything. His word became my command. Of course, it affected me! All this time, every struggle that I came across was created somehow because of the erroneous beliefs in the back of my mind. They were locked away and forgotten but they still made their presence felt. All my life has been about unlearning those wrong lessons whether I knew it or not. Of course, I fell into depression. I once had accepted it all myself.

She was hit by another realization and was amazed to see how a person's past never really leaves and how much of a mystery her own life had been to her. She was no psychiatrist but she could finally see the patterns. How she was left alone by everyone she knew. They all broke her trust one by one as predicted by Swami Ji.

Was it all done to me? Or did I somehow made it happen? By behaving a certain way because I had this strong, ancient belief in my mind that said: The world is a trap!

Was I a victim or was I my own torturer?

I was none.

I was just a little girl...

She stood up from her bed, opened the window and looked at the crescent moon in the sky.

The crescent that is adorned by Shiva, on his head. She wished she had someone to tell all this to; the way she looked at the world, the wonders her own life kept opening to her.

How was it possible? To feel sad for a certain event and then that same event in memory turns into a revolutionary lesson. A lesson of belief.

You make your own beliefs and then the beliefs make you. You are your destiny.

She wanted to share it all with someone, as it came, for the rest of her life. So that she could leave with the knowing that someone heard her, knew her.

Chapter 49

MISS BOLD

"Hi there!"

"Hello! Mr. Madhav," Ray said cheerfully.

"You can call me Madhav."

"Okay…"

Ray had decided to be more open to all the great possibilities that the world had to offer her so she was going with the flow of their conversation…

"You've risen up and my job has only been to simply learn from my dad," Madhav said.

"I don't think that's easy in any way. After all, it's a huge responsibility for anyone. I would think twice before accepting it. I'm more like a go-easy girl. I do things as I go, with my own pace. I don't have a weight on my shoulders."

Literally, not anymore.

"That's really adorable." He kept looking at her.

She looked at him for a second and he didn't look away.

"I guess…" she said intimidated, just a little.

"It's time for you to go?" Madhav said in a low voice.

"Yeah… you're not leaving?"

"No, I'm leaving too."

Ray was about to get inside the car, but Madhav stopped her. "Uh, hey! Um… if you don't mind can we go somewhere next week? After the session of course."

"I'll let you know if it's possible."

Why didn't I just say yes?

"Okay. Bye."

"Bye."

The Universal Economic Forum was being held in her city and all the biggies were present there including Mr. Chandrashekhar who was the guest of honour.

"I expect the young generation to take us farther than we've ever gone. Thank you very much." The business tycoon's thick uvular voice finally rested and he finished his speech. Everyone stood up and applauded him for a good minute.

Ray was stunned to see the amount of respect one could earn. She couldn't help but imagine herself there, in his place someday.

Madhav isn't here?

And then an energetic silhouette appeared to take Mr. Chandrashekhar down the stairs.

There he is.

The after-party began and Mr. Chandrashekhar bid adieu to everyone.

That means Madhav is going too?

Ray was now finding it hard to concentrate on the conversation going on around her.

Why am I even thinking of him. Even if he stays, he will have plenty of company already.

Indeed Madhav was still present and he had plenty of company, mostly women and Ray saw that.

I don't want to be here anymore.

"Excuse me, I have to use the restroom," she excused herself and went to the restroom. Looking at herself in the mirror, she saw that she looked nothing less than a goddess in her yellow v-neck gown which had a little train too. Her hair open, naturally wavy and tousled.

At least I'll have fiery pictures to upload!

Three guys had approached her for a drink earlier in the night and tried to impress her with their estates and bank-balance. A woman in her forties seemed very eager to talk to her. Ray checked carefully if she had followed her to the restroom. Thankfully, she didn't. Losing no time, Ray called her driver to get her car ready to leave.

As she stepped out of the restroom, the woman emerged out of nowhere.

"Oh there you are!" She held her hand and dragged her back to the party.

Ray stopped her midway. "Actually miss, I'm not feeling very well so I want to go," she said without hesitation.

"Oh dear." She put her hand on Ray's face to check her temperature and then squeezed her arm.

Ray somehow managed to not burst out in exasperation. "I really have to go. Take care."

Ray was walking fiercely in her high heels towards the exit.

I don't want to waste another second here.

"Leaving yet?"

Ray couldn't believe the voice that she heard. It calmed her a little but her body was still very much in the rage. She turned in a fierce swing and her hair hit her cheeks. Madhav stood right in front of her with his mouth agape and eyes fixated on her.

"Oh hi, Mr. Madhav, I didn't see you're still here."

"Woah..." escaped from his mouth.

Ray blinked her eyes in confusion.

Madhav regained himself. "Uh yes, I didn't leave. Dad has a very strict sleep schedule so he had to go. But you're leaving?"

"Ah, yes, not feeling well."

"What happened? Can I help you?"

"Nothing, just my mom called me and she's not feeling well so I'm not feeling well."

"O okay, then."

"It was nice meeting you." She left for the exit.

"Uh... hey! Wait!" Madhav caught up with her. "You walk fast."

"Yeah... sometimes." She now cooled down.

"Allow me to drop you home."

Ray looked at him, really looked at him. "Oh no... you don't have to."

"Don't worry, I won't take you anywhere else."

Ray smiled, "I wasn't even thinking that."

"Then what did you think?"

"That you have a lot of people waiting for you here."

Madhav chuckled and Ray cherished.

"I always do. They can wait. Let me drop you home in my car."

Ray let out a sigh and smiled, "Okay."

***

"Your dad is exemplary..." Ray got chills saying that.

"No doubt. Very focused." He was focused on the road.

"Do you feel pressured?"

"Nope actually, I feel good. At home."

"That's great."

"You still have to give me the directions."

"Yeah, keep going," Ray said laughingly.

They both kept quiet for a moment. Ray really seeped in the scene around her. The road, the lights, his cologne, his hands on the steering...

She suddenly looked away, out of the window. "I didn't expect to have such an expensive chauffeur, ever."

"Really? Do you like it?" His voice and smile so sweet.

"I mean, you drive fine but I don't think I can actually afford you." She immediately pursed her lips after saying that.

"Where to go, miss?"

"Right."

"Are you free?"

"Hmm?"

"On Saturday, remember?"

"I guess, yes unless something comes up."

"Okay. Your call. You..."

"Right. You were saying something?"

"Nothing."

"Come on."

"You look pretty," he said, looking straight at the road.

Ray felt her cheeks go warm and for a moment, she couldn't look away from his face in amazement. "Oh... I... thank you very much."

"I didn't make you uncomfortable, did I?"

"No." Ray smiled. Madhav smiled too.

"We're close."

"Okay, miss."

They both stayed quiet until they arrived at her home.

"You have a nice place," he said.

"Not as good as yours. Wait. I've never seen your place," Ray said in one breath.

Madhav smiled to himself. "Don't return compliments too much, you deserve them. And I'll show you my place someday."

"Uh... you don't have to. I mean it's not a—"

"Okay, okay, whenever you want to. Your call."

"Okay..." She didn't look away.

Madhav started to move back but he, too, didn't look away. "See you on the weekend. Take care. Got to go."

"You too." Ray watched his car leave until it disappeared.

"Hey! Rayleena!" Ray looked back identifying the voice.

Rayveena it is.

It was the stormy teenage daughter of their neighbors. She was sitting on her room's window sill with a bottle in her hand.

"What?" Ray shouted back.

"Nice roll Rayleenah… he's hot!" She winked.

"It's Rayveena!"

"You look bomb too, by the way," she said, taking a sip from her water bottle.

"You look bomb too, now don't fall down. Bye." Ray walked towards her house.

Don't return compliments, you deserve them.

The words resonated in her soul.

"GoOoodnIght… Rayleenah…"

***

When did my life change so much? There used to be a time when I used to lie in my bed crying all night. How can things change so much. A 180 degree flip?

You were the one who changed it all. 180.

Yes, I know that. All I ever had was a little belief but where do I go from here, I don't know.

You already know, Ray. You want someone to share it all with.

I don't think I can do that again, to open up to someone completely and then find out about their real intentions. I don't think that anyone can actually love me for me and not for, you know, the surface things.

But that doesn't mean you can't have a little fun. Someone who's so accomplished and big wants to spend time with you. Do you have any idea of how many high profile girls are already after him?

Won't I do the same thing then? Seeing him for his reputation, surface things… I have no fricking idea of who he actually is.

Then get an idea.

Chapter 50

NATURE'S SIMPLICITY

"So? Whatsay?" Madhav asked her flashing his eyebrows.

"You seem to be in a *good mood* today!" Ray observed Madhav and he kept looking at her with one eyebrow raised, eyes squinted and a pleading question on his face.

"I have seen that face before," she said, her eyes narrowed too but Madhav still kept looking. She gave up and said, "Fine. Where are we going?"

"Do you have any place in mind?"

"No I don't go out much," she said in a low voice, in one breath.

"I know just the place. You'll love it." He started walking faster.

"But it should be a quiet one right?"

"Trust me."

"Let's see."

They stopped by a thin and open forest. Ray stepped out of the car and looked around. They were all tall trees which Ray couldn't recognize. The ground was clear and had almost no grass. One could actually see very far through the woods.

"Quiet enough?" he asked.

Ray half-smiled.

Too quiet.

Then she heard chirpings, whistling and contact-calling of birds she had never seen before, singing songs that she had never heard before.

Ray saw the winter sun warming the forest in a lullaby. The trees too, seemed half-awake in the golden light. The whole place seemed to be in an invisible haze that had touched her heart too. Ray felt a pull. She looked to her left, dragging her eyes from the fairytale forest in front of her... to see Madhav looking back at the forest with a longing. Ray thought she was looking at someone too familiar and breathed in. She looked back at the forest, seeing exactly what he was seeing.

"It's so beautiful," she said, awake and hypnotized.

"Indeed," Madhav said, looking at her.

"It doesn't just look beautiful, it feels beautiful," Ray said it like she was arguing.

"It does," he said with a conviction.

Ray kept at least a two feet distance between him and herself as she walked and touched and felt each tree's wrinkles. He walked comfortably, his hands in his jeans pockets.

Ray started to walk backwards with Madhav, while looking up at the sun. She felt like a child. Only a child under the supervision of an adult. She was both.

They didn't say anything for the longest time but kept walking to wherever they felt like. Sometimes, she led him, other times, he led her. Ray was happy that she didn't have to say anything and could take it all in silently. Then she heard water flowing.

"Where is it coming from?"

"There." Madhav pointed to his left.

They both walked in that direction and a cool breeze welcomed them through the trees. It was a river.

"Don't go any further, it's muddy." Madhav stopped her.

"Okay."

They both kept staring at the glory of the river dragon and it's cool, windy wings.

"I love winter, the cold," Ray said with an undeniable smile. She finally let a little bit of her guard down.

"I like winter *and* summer," he objected.

"I don't like summer, it's so... chaotic. My mind doesn't work well during summertime." She swang while sitting on the ground, her arms on her knees.

Madhav laughed, hiding his face.

"What?" She was half-amazed.

"Your mind doesn't work during summer?"

"Not like that, but I mean everything seems so... chaotic as I said."

"I see, you love winter but summer is when you go for a swim in the sea, you wear more open clothes, you enjoy things like sundaes and chilled drinks and ice. Isn't it so?"

"Mm... guess I have to learn to be friends with summer."

"Good for a start. But let's enjoy the winter for now." Madhav kept looking at the river and so did she.

"I'm the only kid to my parents. Mom left us when I was sixteen."

"What do you mean, left?" she asked.

"She's no more."

Ray was silent.

He continued, "I felt bad back then but I knew that my father felt worse so I asked him to get married again but he said that he was married to his work."

"I see… I'm the only kid in my family too and… it's been a… *ride.*"

"Ride? How?"

"I mean, you know, how there's a bias in some people's minds about girls. My parents were the same, they wanted a son. But it's all good now." Ray said without any emotion as she made waves with her finger in the mud.

"Of course, they're happy now seeing their daughter become a multi-millionaire."

"Yes." She really felt the compliment.

"I've grown up seeing my dad's fierce devotion, be it for my mom or for his work and that's what I've inherited from him a little bit. I've never even dated anyone in my entire life."

"Why?!" That was unexpected for her.

"It's not like I didn't have the chance, it's just that I felt too responsible for my dad's hard work and his devotion that I didn't want to make stupid headlines with anyone."

"Yeah… but then, why are you here with me?" Ray couldn't help but ask.

Madhav went silent for a second. "You seemed like a genuinely good person and I thought I should get to know you," he said without thinking twice.

So it was a network thingy.

The Sun was setting and Madhav stood up from the ground.

"Come, let's go now." He offered her a hand and Ray took it.

"I know, I'm heavier than I look. It's called bone density," Ray said, dusting off her jeans.

"Oh please, it was nothing. I'll see you tomorrow?"

"Yeah, won't skip my meditation session."

"Great. Me neither."

***

Ray kept rejoicing the moments from the day. The way he looked at her and the way he even respected her boundaries!

He hasn't even asked for my number...

Ray tried to remember exactly how it felt like to be with him.

"Comfortable... at home... no rushing. But it could be the environment too."

And he didn't break the spell of the environment but added to it right?

I guess...

Chapter 51

UNNAMED, STILL

"You seem quiet today," Madhav said, noticing a quiet Ray.

"No. I'm good." Ray wasn't even looking at him.

"If something's bothering you… you can tell me."

Ray thought about it a little but then she didn't want to. "I… look, I really need to know why you talk to me. Is it a friendship or a professional relationship that you want to create..?" She caught some breath.

Madhav didn't say anything.

"Okay, let me tell you why I'm asking this. I'm not someone to fool around okay. I can't give my time to anything that's temporary. I hate passing time with anyone. So just, let me know what is it that you want from me?"

"You. I want to know you. That's what I said before," he said in a melting voice.

Ray's face softened but she still needed an answer.

"So you want to know me? Why?"

"I don't know. I just do."

Ray still didn't get what she was looking for.

"Okay, fine, just let it go."

"You don't like being with me?" he asked.

"It's not like that, I just don't want to… listen, it's really hard, really, really hard for me to talk to someone for no reason at all. I can't trust people. I know, not everyone is the same but I just really need to know what is it that you want from me. I can't just **be** with you. You see?

Madhav was lost in contemplation.

Ray was bewildered and gave up. "I just want to go home. I'm sorry if I said anything hurtful."

"Do you want me to drop you off?" he asked soothingly.

"No, no. It's fine."

Ray came back and locked herself in her room. She hid her face in her pillow so that her parents could not listen to her sobs.

"Great, now he won't talk to me again. This time… I've ruined it for myself."

But if he really wants to be with you, he'll understand.

Chapter 52

ANGELS HAVE NIGHTMARES TOO

Hiding behind a tree in an autumn evening,

I saw him.

Walked towards, to see more of him.

I saw a sun glowing without any shame.

And I walked to the sun half-believing,

Looking back at the prying eyes in the trees,

I was beyond myself and happy to see,

Him flying in the glow.

I don't know when he touched me or I did?

But suddenly, it was all golden

And I, with wings just like him.

The next weekend, Ray woke up and opened the door to find lavenders everywhere around the house.

So they remembered, how unusual.

She approached the table to find a freshly baked chocolate cake with no frosting at all.

"Happy Birthday Dear," mom said.

"Happy Birthday," dad followed up with a smile.

"Thank you mom, dad." Ray was really touched. She wasn't really expecting it.

"We made the cake just in time," mom said cheerfully. Her dad stood behind with a little smile.

"It looks perfect, really." Ray was almost tearful.

They arranged the candles and Ray blew them to the birthday song.

"What did you wish for?" mom asked enthusiastically.

"Nothing... I have everything and more. And I'm grateful for it."

"Is there anything that we can give you?" dad asked meekly.

"No, dad really, this cake is everything. You two made it together. It's the most beautiful present." She tried to read his face.

"What can we even give you dear, you have done it all for yourself, we have nothing to give you." Mom hid her face in her hands.

"Mom... if you cry, I won't eat it."

"Okay, okay." She wiped her tears and smiled. "I wish you find a nice guy to marry you. Soon."

A few moments later...

"Ray..! A car is standing outside, it's very big," mom loudly while Ray was in the bathroom.

"I don't know," she shouted back.

"You should come out and see."

Ray came out in her bathrobe to look from the window. "Madhav... no way, what's he doing here?"

Ray came down the stairs not caring about her dripping wet hair.

She stood on the gate for a second to really see whose car it was. It was him. She approached the car and the car window opened. He was wearing his stunning aviators and his hair, slicked back!

Ray smiled at the sight of him as she walked noisily in her wet flip-flops, swinging her arms carefully to keep herself from slipping.

Madhav came out of his car in all his glory holding a balloon and a box in his hands.

"Happy Birthday Rayveena..." he said it like he meant it.

"But, how did you know?" She winked several times in amazement.

"You ask too many questions. You have a richymedia page, you know that?"

"Oh."

"Here, it's for you. Do tell me how it tastes, made it myself."

"What? No way. I mean, thank you so much. Why don't you come inside?" she pleaded.

"Oh actually, you see, I have to go for work." He pointed at himself.

"Okay, then." Ray was a little disappointed.

"Then, enjoy your day, Ray."

"For sure." She looked at the golden balloon and the box. "Hey... but wait, how will I tell you how it tasted?"

"Oh yeah, give me your number, well, if you want to."

"Okay, give me your phone." Ray gave him the balloon to hold for a second.

He looks so out of character like this,

she smiled to herself.

"What?" He was clueless.

"Nothing, here." She handed him the phone back and took the balloon back into her authority.

"Enjoy," he said.

"You too."

Ray went inside and met her mom's wide open eyes.

"What?" Ray asked her aloud and went straight to her room. Mom's mouth still agape.

Ray opened the box and it smelled so good. She picked up a little piece with her fingers and smelled it again.

Cheers!

It was delicious. She decided to eat the cake piece by piece throughout the day, without sharing.

"It's delicious. Thank you so much," Ray texted Madhav.

"I'm glad. Happy Birthday again... Enjoy."

Ray fell down on her bed. "I'm in heaven... Happy Birthday Ray!"

***

Ray was expecting to sleep soundly given the fact that she had a great birthday and that, too, with the people she wanted to spend it with. It was the world to her.

But she woke up from a nightmare at midnight.

She saw a little girl crying alone and everyone around her just looked at her and went about their business. She was sitting on the ground, wiping her soaring tears.

To see her like that, was heartbreaking. Suddenly, Ray saw an adult man come running in her direction out of nowhere, to hit the girl. Ray rushed to her and saved her just in time. She held her in her arms, close to her heart to stop her sobbing.

Ray sat up agitated. She slowed down her breathing and calmed her waning heart.

Why this dream? Why? Everything is going right in my life. Then?

And it hit her.

The girl is me. And I have to save me. I never want to go back to that place of sorrow. Never going back to all that I went through. I can't stay waiting like this either.

Chapter 53

LOVE

The Queen finds her reign in the arms of her true King only.

Madhav and Rayveena have been together for a year now. They had even started a couple of new successful business ventures together and were being dubbed a **power couple** by the paparazzi. They were going around the world together, having the best of everything together.

phewweepheww Ray whistled at the sight of him.

Madhav looked up at her as he removed his tie while Ray devoured her man with her eyes.

He started to walk towards her, rolling his white shirt's cuffs. She, in a full sleeves, high neck bodycon dress, watched him walk; her hands behind her back.

"Seriously, if I had known that you are such a—" he threatened.

"What?" She grabbed him by the collar and pulled him closer. "Say," she whispered.

Madhav lifted her up in his arms. "Such a..."

"Hmm?"

"Mine."

"What?" she asked, laughing.

"Mine. You're mine," he said looking deep into her soul.

"No, you're mine." Ray stared into his eyes and she clasped his hand with hers. He spun her in air once and put her back on the floor. He put his hands on her waist and she lingered her fingers on his shoulders.

"You're so beautiful," Ray whispered as she reached for his lips. He leaned in and planted a passionate kiss on hers.

"You're the most beautiful woman I've ever seen."

And he went all in and didn't stop himself and neither did Ray. He suddenly stopped in between the kiss and parted from her. She kept looking at him with a longing, the same that he had.

"I have to do this. Doesn't matter." He started to get down on his right knee.

Ray's breath had stopped and her mind was filled with a million questions.

Is it too soon? Am I ready? What will I say? Do I really love him? What if it's just our hormones? Ugh!

In the same moment, came the answers running to her:

I've waited enough. No one is ever ready. Say what's on your heart. You chose to trust him and that was the bravest thing you did. Not everyone lights up your hormones.

The glass window let in a soft evening glow. Madhav looked like an angel in it. His hair, glowing like a halo. When Madhav got comfortable, he took her left hand in his hands and kissed it with his eyes closed.

She dropped down on one knee in an instant and looked at him in a way she had never looked at anyone before. Her breath was heavy and her heart filled with an emotion that she had waited for forever.

Live this moment.

She let go of every control on her senses and was fully in the moment.

Madhav seemed like he was holding a river behind his eyes. He snorted and swallowed. "You know I love you, right?" he asked and Ray nodded with a smile, holding his hand tighter.

"Let me tell you something... the first time that I saw you, it was a speech of yours. I was there, by the way."

"What?" Ray smiled in surprise.

"Listen to me, the first time that I saw you, I was... awestruck. Your voice soothed my ears in a way that nothing ever did. Your demeanour, your gestures, everything about you looked so powerful and magical at the same time."

Ray breathed in deeply, so did he.

"I... wanted to know you and I found out that you have a heart of gold no, diamond and your skin is so soft!"

They both chuckled and cherished.

"And I just knew that I had to be with you. I know it's very hard for you to trust anyone and I'm not saying that I'm perfect but I can say this, I will love you forever, there will never be anything that you won't have. And if I had to leave it all, I will leave it all to be with you."

"Me too," Ray said in an instant.

"If my ego ever got between us, I will accept every punishment of yours. You will have all the power in this."

"Hey, easy, Madhav..." She played with his fingers.

"Okay, let's do this. Miss Rayveena, I love you with every bit of me... will you give me the honour of your company, in everything that I do, for the rest of my life?"

Ray felt emotions that she had never felt before, she was so lost in his face that it took a moment to realize that he was waiting for an answer.

"Yes," Ray said without blinking.

Madhav took a deep breath and closed his eyes. "Okay now, I will say this."

"Just say it."

"Miss Rayveena, will you marry me?"

Time seemed to stop and they both looked at each other trying to read eyes.

"Yes, my love. Yes. I will." They embraced each other so badly that they lost their balance and rolled on the floor.

"Hey wait, wait, wait." Madhav suddenly sat back up, rolling Ray aside.

"What?"

"We need to get back in position."

"WHY?!"

Madhav gave her a hand and Ray sat herself up as she was before, Madhav too.

They both were on their knees. Again.

"What?" Ray said, loving his stupidity. Madhav reached out with his free hand to his back pocket and pulled out a golden heart-shaped ring box. He held it carefully and opened it in front of her.

Ray was mesmerized by the white gold band which had a head shaped like a queen's crown with diamonds all around the top portions and in the halo of it, sat a brilliant 50-carat, heart-cut diamond.

"To the Queen of my Heart. I know, cheesy but I mean it." Madhav had loosened up.

Ray really took in the beauty of that beast of a diamond and then she looked up at him and all the brilliance of the diamond was lost in front of this person's aura. "You're more brilliant than any diamond, Madhav."

He smiled shyly and held her left hand. "Now, I'm going to put this diamond on your finger. Are you ready?"

"Are you?"

Madhav kissed her hand once and then slid the ring slowly.

Ray looked at her hand. "This isn't real."

And they hugged each other like they had never before. Madhav kissed her head, holding her tight in his arms. Ray had nothing she wanted anymore. She felt complete.

"I love you, Madhav. Forever."

"I love you an infinity and back."

"I love you an infinity squared and back."

"I love you a big bang to the power of infinity and back."

"Okay! I got the idea."

They both laughed in sync.

"... And by the way, I got my pilot's license today..." She flashed her eyebrows twice.

Madhav pulled her closer and whispered in her ear, "Then let's fly to heaven... **NOW!**"

About The Author

Jyoti Singh has been a student of Mechanical Engineering and she has been around. In search of her calling, she has had short-lived flings with first, real estate then, journalism and now, she is merrily committed to literature.

Feel free to share your thoughts. ☺

Email: jedi797@gmail.com

www.ingramcontent.com/pod-product-compliance
Lightning Source LLC
LaVergne TN
LVHW040115180726

843489LV00005B/1421